This book belongs to

CONTRIBUTORS

Illustrated by
Alison Atkins, Andrew Geeson, Andy Everitt Stewart,
Anglea Kincaid, Anna Cynthia Leplar, Caroline Davis,
Claire Henley, Claire Mumford, Daniel Howarth,
Dorothy Clark, Elaine Keary, Frank Endersby,
Georgia Birkett, Gillian Roberts, Jacqueline East,
Jacqueline Mair, Jan Lewis, Jane Molineaux,
Jane Swift, Jane Tattersfield, Jessica Stockham,
Jo Brown, Julie Nicholson, Karen Perrins, Kate Aldous,
Kate Davies, Linda Worrell, Liz Pichon, Louise Gardner,
Maggie Downer, Mario Capaldi, Martin Grant, Nicola Evans,
Paula Martyr, Peter Rutherford, Piers Harper, Rebecca Elgar,
Rikki O'Neill, Rory Tyger, Sara Walker, Scott Rhodes,
Serena Feneziani, Sheila Moxley, Stephanie Boey, Sue Clarke,
Terry Burton, Pauline Siewart, Lorna Bannister

Written by
Nicola Baxter, Janet Allison Brown, Andrew Charman, Jillian
Harker, Heather Henning, Alistair Hedley, Claire Keen,
Ronne Randall, Lesley Rees, Caroline Repchuk, Kay Barnes,
Gaby Goldsack, Aneurin Rhys, Louisa Somerville, Derek Hall,
Marilyn Tolhurst, Alison Morris, Nicola Edwards,
Jackie Andrews

# STORYTIME TALES

A Keepsake Treasury

Every effort has been made to acknowledge the
contributors to this book. If we have made any errors,
we will be pleased to rectify them in future editions.

This is a Parragon Book
This edition published in 2003

Parragon
Queen Street House
4 Queen Street
Bath BA1 1HE, UK

Design and project management by Aztec Design

Page make-up by Mik Martin and Caroline Reeves

ISBN 1-40540-291-1
Printed in China

# STORYTIME TALES

A Keepsake Treasury

$p$

# Contents

# CONTENTS

# ❧ CONTENTS ❧

# Cinderella

Once upon a time, there lived a very pretty girl. Sadly, when she was young, her mother died. Her father remarried, but the girl's stepmother was a mean woman with two ugly daughters. These stepsisters were so jealous of the young girl's beauty that they treated her like a servant and made her sit among the cinders in the kitchen.

They called her Cinderella, and before long everyone, even her father, had forgotten the poor girl's real name. Cinderella missed her real mother more and more each day.

One day, an invitation arrived from the royal palace. The king and queen were holding a ball for the prince's twenty-first birthday, and all the fine ladies of the kingdom were invited.

Cinderella's stepsisters were very excited when their invitations to the ball arrived.

"I will wear my red velvet gown!" cried the first stepsister. "And the black pearl necklace that Mother gave to me."

"And I will wear my blue silk dress with a silver tiara!" cried the other.

"Come, Cinderella!" they called. "You must help us to get ready!"

Cinderella helped her stepsisters with their silk stockings and frilly petticoats. She brushed and curled their hair and powdered their cheeks and noses. At last, she squeezed them into their beautiful ball-gowns. But, even after all this, the two ugly stepsisters weren't nearly as lovely as Cinderella was in her rags. This made them very jealous and angry, and they began to tease Cinderella.

"Too bad you can't come with us, Cinders!" sneered the first stepsister.

"Yes," laughed the other one. "They'd never let a shabby creature like you near the palace!"

Cinderella said nothing, but inside, her heart was breaking. She really wanted to go to the ball. After her stepsisters left, she sat and wept.

"Dry your tears, my dear," said a gentle voice.

Cinderella was amazed. A kind old woman stood before her. In her hand was a sparkly wand that shone.

"I am your fairy godmother," she told Cinderella. "And you shall go to the ball!"

"But I have nothing to wear! How will I get there?" cried Cinderella.

The fairy godmother smiled at Cinderella.

The fairy godmother asked Cinders to fetch her the biggest pumpkin in the garden. With a flick of her magic wand she turned it into a golden carriage and the mice in the kitchen mousetrap into fine horses. A fat rat soon became a handsome coachman.

Cinderella could not believe her eyes.

Then the fairy godmother waved her wand once more and suddenly Cinderella was dressed in a splendid ball-gown. On her feet were sparkling glass slippers.

"My magic will end at midnight, so you must be home before then," said the fairy godmother. "Good luck."

When Cinderella arrived at the ball, everyone was dazzled by her beauty. Whispers went round the ballroom as the other guests wondered who this enchanting stranger could be. Even Cinderella's own stepsisters did not recognise her.

As soon as the prince set eyes on Cinderella, he fell in love with her. "Would you do me the honour of this dance?" he asked.

"Why certainly, sir," Cinderella answered. And from that moment on he only had eyes for Cinderella.

Soon the clock struck midnight. "I must go!" said Cinderella, suddenly remembering her promise to her fairy godmother. She fled from the ballroom and ran down the palace steps. The prince ran after her, but when he got outside, she was gone. He didn't notice a grubby servant girl holding a pumpkin. A few mice and a rat scurried around her feet.

But there on the steps was one dainty glass slipper. The prince picked it up and rushed back into the palace. "Does anyone know who this slipper belongs to?" he cried.

The next day, Cinderella's stepsisters talked of nothing but the ball,

and the beautiful stranger who had danced all night with the prince. As they were talking, there was a knock at the door.

"Cinderella," called the stepmother, "quick, jump to it and see who it is." Standing on the doorstep was the prince and a royal footman, who was holding the little glass slipper on a velvet cushion.

"The lady whose foot this slipper fits is my one and only true love," said the prince. "I am going to visit every house in the kingdom in search of her."

The two stepsisters began shoving each other out of the way in their rush to try on the slipper. They both squeezed and pushed as hard as they could, but their clumsy feet were far too big for the tiny glass shoe.

Then Cinderella stepped forward. "Please, Your Highness," she said, shyly, "may I try?"

As her stepsisters watched in utter amazement, Cinderella slid her foot into the dainty slipper. It fitted as if it were made for her!

As the prince gazed into her eyes, he knew he had found his love – and Cinderella knew she had found hers.

Cinderella and the prince soon set a date to be married.

On the day of their wedding, the land rang to the sound of bells, and the sun shone as the people cheered. Even Cinderella's nasty stepsisters were invited. Everyone had a really wonderful day, and Cinderella and her prince lived happily ever after.

# Webster the Littlest Frog

Webster was the littlest frog on the pond, and he was fed up. Fed up with being bossed about. Fed up with playing on his own. Fed up, in fact, with being the littlest frog. None of the bigger frogs would let Webster play games with them.

"Hop it, Titch!" they croaked. "You're far too small to join our games."

Every day, Webster sat on his own, watching the other frogs play leap-frog on Looking-Glass Pond.

"You don't have to be a big frog to jump," thought Webster, as he watched. "I can do that."

At last, one bright, moonlit night, Webster found the courage to ask if he could join in.

"Please let me play with you," said Webster. "I can jump really high!"

The other frogs just laughed.

"But I can!" he insisted. He took a deep breath. "I can jump... over the moon!"

The other frogs laughed so much, they nearly fell off their lily pads.

"I'll prove it!" he said. "Just watch me."

One... two... three... JUMP! Webster leapt off his lily pad and sailed over the moon's reflection in the pond.

The other frogs stared in amazement. It was true. Webster could jump over the moon!

"We're sorry we didn't believe you," said one of the big frogs.

"Please play with us! You might not be the biggest frog on the pond, but you certainly are the cleverest!"

# Just as Well Really

**R**umpus liked water. He liked the drippiness and droppiness, the splashiness and sloppiness of it!

He liked it so much that, whenever there was water around, Rumpus somehow always managed to fall into it!

But Mum loved Rumpus, so every time she simply sighed and she mopped up the mess.

Rumpus loved mud. He loved the way you could plodge in it, splodge in it, slide in it and glide in it! Rumpus somehow always managed to get covered in it!

But Dad loved Rumpus, so every time he simply sighed and he sponged off the splatters.

Rumpus enjoyed paint. He liked to splatter and dash it, to spread and splash it! Rumpus somehow managed to get it everywhere!

But Rumpus' brother loved him, so every time he simply sighed and cleaned himself up.

Rumpus liked to find out how things worked. He loved the prodding and probing, the wiggling and the jiggling, the unscrewing and the undoing!

He loved it so much that, whenever Rumpus was around, things didn't work for long!

But Granny loved Rumpus, so she simply sighed and she tidied away the clutter.

Rumpus loved his mum, dad, brother and granny. Rumpus' mum, dad, brother and granny all loved Rumpus... just as well, really!

# The Frog Prince

There was once a king who had but one daughter. Being his only child, she wanted for nothing. She had a nursery full of toys, her own pony to ride and a wardrobe bursting with pretty dresses. But, for all this, the princess was lonely. "How I wish I had someone to play with," she sighed.

The princess's favourite toy was a beautiful golden ball. Every day she would play with her ball in the palace garden. When she threw the ball up in the air, it seemed to take off of its own accord and touch the clouds before landing safely in the princess's hands again.

One windy day the princess was playing in the garden as usual. She threw her golden ball high into the air, but, instead of returning to her hands, the wind blew the ball into the fishpond. The princess ran to the pond, but to her dismay the ball had sunk right to the bottom. "Whatever shall I do?" wailed the girl. "Now I have lost my favourite toy." And she sat down by the pond and cried.

All at once she heard a loud PLOP! and a large green frog landed on the grass beside her. "Eeek! Go away you nasty thing!" screamed the princess.

To her astonishment, the frog spoke to her. "I heard you crying," he said in a gentle voice, "and I wondered what was wrong. Can I help you?"

"Why, yes!" exclaimed the princess, once she had got over the shock of being addressed by a frog. "My ball has sunk to the bottom of the pond. Would you fish it out for me?"

"Of course I will," replied the frog. "But in return, what will you give me?"

"You can have my jewels, my finest clothes and even my crown if you will find my ball," said the princess hastily, for she was truly eager to get her favourite toy back.

"I do not want your jewels, your clothes or your crown," replied the frog. "I would like to be your friend. I want to return with you to the palace and eat from your golden plate and sip from your golden cup. At night I want to sleep on a cushion made of silk next to your bed and I want you to kiss me goodnight before I go to sleep, too."

"I promise everything that you ask," said the girl, "if only you will find my golden ball."

"Remember what you have promised," said the frog, as he dived deep into the pond. At last he surfaced again with the ball and threw it on to the grass beside the princess. She was so overjoyed she forgot all about thanking the frog – let alone her promise – and ran all the way back to the palace.

That evening the king, the queen and the princess were having dinner in the great hall of the palace, when a courtier whispered to the king. "Your Majesty, there is a frog at the door who says the princess has promised to share her dinner with him."

"Is this true?" demanded the king, turning angrily to the princess.

"Yes, it is," said the princess in a small voice. And she told her father the whole story.

"When a promise is made it must be kept, my girl," said the king. "You must ask the frog to dine with you."

Presently, the frog hopped into the great hall. With a great leap he was up on the table beside the princess. She stifled a scream.

"You promised to let me eat from your golden plate and sip from your golden cup," said the frog, tucking into the princess's food. The princess felt sick and pushed the plate away from her. When he had finished, the frog stretched his long, green limbs, yawned and said, "Now I feel quite sleepy. Please take me to your room."

"Do I really have to?" the princess pleaded with her father.

"Yes, you do," said the king sternly. "The frog helped you when you were in need and you made him a promise."

So the princess carried the frog to her bedroom. As they reached the door she said, "My bedroom is very warm. I'm sure you'd be more comfortable out here where it's cool."

But, as she opened the bedroom door, the frog leaped from her hand and landed on her bed.

"You promised that I could sleep on a silk cushion next to your bed," said the frog.

"Yes, yes, of course," said the princess looking with horror at the froggy footprints on her clean, white sheets. She called to her maid to bring a cushion.

The frog jumped on to the cushion and looked as though he was going to sleep. But then he opened his eyes and said, "What about my goodnight kiss?"

"Oh, woe is me!" thought the princess as she closed her eyes and pursed her lips towards the frog's cold and clammy face and kissed him.

"Open your eyes," said a voice that didn't sound a bit like the frog's. She opened her eyes and there, standing before her, was a prince. The princess stood there in dumbstruck amazement.

"Thank you," said the prince. "You have broken a spell cast upon me by a wicked witch. I became a frog and the spell could only be broken if a princess would eat with me, sleep beside me and kiss me."

They ran to tell the king what had happened. He was delighted and said, "You may live in the palace from now on, for my daughter needs a friend." And, indeed, the prince and princess became the best of friends and she was never lonely again. He taught her to play football with the golden ball and she taught him to ride her pony. One day, many years later, they were married and had lots of children. And, do you know, their children were particularly good at leapfrog!

# Sugarplum
## and the
# Butterfly

"Sugarplum," said the Fairy Queen, "I've got a very important job for you to do." Sugarplum was always given the most important work. The Fairy Queen said it was because she was the kindest and most helpful of all the fairies. "I want you to make a rose-petal ball gown for my birthday ball next week."

Sugarplum began to gather cobwebs for the thread, and rose petals for the dress. While she was collecting the thread she found a butterfly caught in a cobweb.

Carefully, Sugarplum untangled the butterfly, but his wing was broken. Sugarplum laid the butterfly on a bed of feathers, then she gathered nectar from a special flower and fed him a drop at a time. Then she set about mending his wing with a magic spell.

After six days, the butterfly was better. He was very grateful. But now Sugarplum was behind with her work!

"Oh dear! I shall never finish the Fairy Queen's ball gown by tomorrow," she cried. "Whatever shall I do?" The butterfly comforted her.

"Don't worry, Sugarplum," he said. "We'll help you." He gathered all his friends together and told them how Sugarplum had rescued him from the cobweb and helped to mend his wing.

The butterflies gathered up lots of rose petals and cobwebs. Back and forth went Sugarplum's hand with her needle and thread making the finest cobweb stitches. When she had finished, Sugarplum was very pleased. "Dear friend," she said to the butterfly, "I couldn't have finished the dress without your help."

"And I could never have flown again without your kindness and help," said the butterfly.

The Fairy Queen was delighted with her new ball gown. And, when she heard the butterfly's story, she wrote a special Thank You poem for Sugarplum:

Sugarplum is helpful,
   Sugarplum is kind.
Sugarplum works hard all day,
   But she doesn't mind.
She always does her very best,
   To make sick creatures well.
She brings such joy and pleasure
   As she weaves her magic spell!

# Wonky Bear

Mr and Mrs Puppety owned an old-fashioned toy shop. They made toys by hand in a room at the back of the shop. But they were getting old and their eyesight was bad.

"It's time we got an apprentice toymaker," said Mr Puppety to his wife. They soon found a young lad called Tom to work for them. He worked hard and carefully. He spent his first week making a teddy bear. When he had finished he showed the bear to Mr and Mrs Puppety.

"He looks very happy and cuddly," said Mrs Puppety.

Tom was very pleased that they liked his first bear and he went off home whistling happily.

"He really is a lovely bear," said Mr Puppety, "but his head is a bit wonky."

"I know," said his wife, "but it's Tom's first try. Let's just put him up there on the shelf with the other teddy bears."

That night Wonky Bear sat on the shelf and started to cry. He had heard what Mr and Mrs Puppety had said about him.

"What's wrong?" asked Brown Bear, who was sitting next to him.

"My head is on wonky," sobbed Wonky Bear.

"But does it hurt?" asked Brown Bear.

"No," replied Wonky Bear.

"Well then, why are you crying?" asked Brown Bear.

"Because nobody will want to buy a wonky bear. I shall be left here forever and nobody will ever take me home and love me," he cried.

"Don't worry," said Brown Bear. "We've all got our faults, but you look fine to me. Just try your best to look cute and cuddly and you'll soon have someone to love you." This made Wonky Bear feel much happier and he fell fast asleep.

The next day the shop was full of people, but nobody paid any attention to Wonky Bear. Then a little boy looked up at the shelf and cried, "Oh, what a lovely bear. Can I have that one, Daddy?"

Wonky Bear's heart lifted as the little boy's daddy reached up to his shelf. But he picked up Brown Bear instead and handed him to the little boy. Wonky Bear felt sadder than ever. Nobody wanted him. All of his new friends would get sold and leave the shop, but he would be left on the shelf gathering dust. Poor old Wonky Bear!

Now, Mr and Mrs Puppety had a little granddaughter called Jessie who loved to visit the shop and play with the toys. All the toys loved her because she was gentle and kind. It so happened that the next time she came to visit it was her birthday, and her grandparents told her she could choose any toy she wanted as her present.

"I know she won't choose me," thought Wonky Bear sadly. "Not with all these other beautiful toys to choose from."

But, to Wonky's amazement, Jessie looked up and pointed at his shelf and said, "I'd like that wonky bear please. No one else will have a bear quite like him."

Mr Puppety smiled and gave Wonky to Jessie. She hugged and kissed him, and Wonky felt so happy he almost cried. She took him home and put a smart red bow around his neck ready for her birthday party. He felt very proud indeed.

Soon the other children arrived, each carrying their teddy bears under their arms.

Wonky Bear could not believe his eyes when he saw the little boy with his friend Brown Bear!

"I'm having a teddy bears' picnic," Jessie explained to him, hugging him tight. All of the children and the bears had a wonderful time, especially Wonky. He had found a lovely home, met his old friend and made lots of new ones.

"See, I told you not to worry," said Brown Bear.

"I know," said Wonky. "And I never will again."

# Like a Duck to Water

**M**rs Duck swam proudly across the farm pond followed by a line of fluffy ducklings. Hidden in the safety of the nest, Dozy Duckling peeked out and watched them go. He wished he was brave enough to go with them but he was afraid of the water!

When they returned that night they told him tales of all the scary animals they had met by the pond.

"There's a big thing with hot breath called Horse," said Dotty.

"There's a huge smelly pink thing called Pig," said Dickie.

"But worst of all," said Doris, "there's a great grey bird, called Heron. Pig says he gobbles up little ducklings for breakfast!"

Next morning, Mrs Duck hurried the ducklings out for their morning parade. Dozy kept his eyes shut until they had gone, then looked up to see a great grey bird towering over him! He leapt into the water crying, "Help, wait for me!" But the others started laughing!

"It's a trick! Heron won't eat you. We just wanted you to come swimming. And you've taken to it like a duck to water!"

# Bear Finds a Friend

Sally found the teddy bear in the park. It was a small, light brown bear, wearing pale blue dungarees and a red and white striped shirt. "Look, Mum," said Sally, "There's a teddy here. What shall we do with it?"

"We'd better take it home with us," said Mum. "We'll put a notice up to say we found it." Sally made a notice and Mum helped her to spell the words. Then she brushed the leaves from the bear and sat it next to her own teddy. She put her teddy's arm round it. "Look after him," she told her teddy. "He must be feeling very frightened."

Sally and Mum took the notice to the park, and pinned it to a tree near the playground. "Now we'll have to wait and see," said Mum.

The telephone rang just before tea time. "Yes, you can come and get it straightaway," Mum said. Five minutes later the doorbell rang and a small girl was standing on the step with her mother. She smiled at Sally, "Thank you for looking after my teddy," she said.

"He made friends with my teddy," said Sally. The girl picked up her bear and hugged him tight.

"Perhaps we could be friends, too," she said.

# Bear's Picnic

Ellie, her brother Alex, and Ellie's teddy bear were playing hide and seek in a wood. "Sit quietly," said Ellie to her teddy, as she placed him behind a tree. "Alex won't find you there." Then she hid too.

"Time to pack up the picnic things," called Ellie's mother. "We need to hurry before it starts to rain." Ellie and Alex collected the plates and cups.

"Race you back to the car," yelled Alex, charging off through the trees.

"I can beat you!" cried Ellie, following. But no one thought of Teddy.

Teddy sat under the tree. A huge leaf drifted down, and landed in front of him. A squirrel dropped the nut he was carrying, and it plopped down onto the leaf in front of the bear. High above, a bird dropped a blackberry from its beak and it fell down onto the leaf, too.

"We've forgotten Teddy!" screamed Ellie as they began to climb into the car. So Ellie and Alex raced back to the tree.

"Look," said Ellie, peering round the tree. "Here he is. He stayed behind to eat his own picnic." She hugged her teddy bear tightly.

"We'll take your plate home with us," she smiled, picking up the leaf.

# Rapunzel

Once upon a time there lived a couple who, after many years, found they were expecting a baby.

Their tiny cottage stood next to a river. Across the river was a beautiful garden full of glorious flowers and tasty-looking vegetables. One day, the woman looked across the river and saw a vegetable called rampion growing in the garden. It looked delicious, and she longed to taste it. She begged her husband to get some.

The garden belonged to an evil witch, and he refused. But his wife would eat nothing else, and grew thin and pale. At last he agreed.

That night, the man crossed the river, entered the witch's garden and picked handfuls of rampion. Suddenly, the evil witch appeared. "How dare you steal from me!" she roared.

"F-Forgive me," the man stammered. "My wife is expecting a baby and longed for some of this vegetable. If she doesn't have it, I'm afraid she will die."

"Very well," said the witch, "take all you want. But you must give me something in return. When your baby is born, I must have it."

Terrified, the man agreed and fled.

The wife was overjoyed and made a salad with the rampion. She ate it hungrily.

After that, the man went to the witch's garden every day. He brought home baskets full of rampion for his wife, and she grew strong and healthy. A few months later she gave birth to a beautiful baby girl.

The man had forgotten all about his promise to the witch, but when the baby was just a day old, she burst in and took her away. The baby's parents were heartbroken and never saw her or the witch again.

The witch called the baby Rapunzel. She took her to a cottage deep in a forest, and took good care of her.

On Rapunzel's twelfth birthday, the witch imprisoned her in a forbidding high tower, with no doors and just one small window at the very top.

Every day the witch stood at the bottom of the tower, and called:
*"Rapunzel, Rapunzel!*
*Let down your long hair!"*

Rapunzel would let down her long, golden hair, and the witch would begin to climb up.

Rapunzel spent many lonely years in her tower. To pass the time, she often sat by the window and sang. One day, a prince rode through the forest. Enchanted by the sound of Rapunzel's sweet voice, the young prince followed it until he came to the doorless tower.

Just then the witch arrived. The prince quickly hid as she called:
*"Rapunzel, Rapunzel!*
*Let down your long hair!"*

The witch began to climb the hair, and the prince knew that this was the way he would be able to meet the owner of the beautiful voice.

After the witch had gone, the prince stood beneath the tower and called in a voice like the witch's:

*"Rapunzel, Rapunzel!*
*Let down your long hair!"*

When Rapunzel's golden hair came tumbling down, he climbed up to the window.

Rapunzel was frightened when she saw the prince. But he was gentle and kind, and she quickly lost her fear.

The prince came to see Rapunzel often, and they soon fell in love. He asked her to marry him – but how would Rapunzel leave the tower?

Rapunzel had an idea. "Each time you visit," she told the prince, "bring me a ball of strong silk. I will plait it into a long, long ladder. When it is finished I will climb down and run away to marry you."

The prince did as Rapunzel asked, and soon the ladder was ready.

But, on the day she was to run away, something terrible happened.

When the witch climbed through the window, Rapunzel absent-mindedly asked, "Why do you pull so hard at my hair? The prince is not so rough."

Suddenly, Rapunzel realised what she had said.

The witch flew into a raging fury. "You ungrateful little wretch!" she screamed. "I have protected you from the world, and you have betrayed me. Now you must be punished!"

"I'm very sorry," Rapunzel sobbed, as she fell to her knees. "I didn't mean to make you cross."

The witch grabbed a pair of scissors and – snip-snap-snip-snap – cut off Rapunzel's long golden hair. Then, using the ladder to climb down, the witch carried Rapunzel off to a faraway land, where she left her to wander all alone without any food, water or anything to keep her warm.

That evening, when the prince called, the witch let down Rapunzel's hair. The prince climbed up quickly, and couldn't believe his eyes!

"The bird has flown, my pretty!" the witch cackled evilly. "You will never see Rapunzel again!"

Overcome with grief, the sad prince threw himself from the tower. His fall was broken by some brambles, but they also scratched and blinded him.

The prince stumbled away and wandered the land for a year, living on berries and rain water.

Then one day the prince heard a beautiful sound drifting through the trees – the sweet voice of Rapunzel!

He called her name and she ran into his arms, weeping tears of joy. The tears fell onto the prince's wounded eyes and suddenly he could see again.

The prince took Rapunzel home to his castle, where they were married and lived happily ever after.

# Leo Makes a Friend

L eo was quite a shy lion. Sometimes he was sad because he didn't have any friends.

"Mum," he said one day, "why will no one play with me?"

"They think you're frightening because you're a lion," said Mum.

One sunny day Leo decided it would be a good day to make a friend. He came to some trees where some small monkeys were playing. When the monkeys saw Leo they scampered to the top of the tallest trees.

"Hello," called out Leo. There was no answer. "Hello," he called again. "Won't you come down and play with me?"

"Go away," one monkey said rudely, "we don't like lions! Your teeth are too big," said the monkey, and giggled noisily.

Leo walked on until he came to a deep pool where a hippopotamus and her baby were bathing.

"Hi!" called out Leo. "Can I come in the water with you? I'd like to play," said Leo.

"So would I!" said Baby Hippo.

"No, you wouldn't," said Mummy Hippo firmly. "You don't play with lions. They have a very loud roar."

Puzzled, Leo walked on. He saw a snake sunbathing on a rock. He touched the snake gently with his paw. "Play with me," he said.

"Ouch!" said the snake. "Your claws are too sharp."

Suddenly, he heard a small voice say, "Hello!"

Leo looked round. He could see a pair of yellow eyes peeping at him from behind a tree. "You won't want to play with me," said Leo grumpily, "I've got a loud roar, and sharp claws, *and* big teeth!"

"So have I," said the voice.

"What are you?" asked Leo.

"I'm a lion, of course!"

And into the clearing walked another little lion.

"I'm a lion, too," said Leo, grinning. "Would you like to share my picnic?"

"Yes, please!" said the other lion. They ate the picnic and played for the rest of the afternoon.

"I like being a lion," said Leo happily. He had made a friend at last!

# The Princess and the Pea

Once upon a time, there was a prince whose dearest wish was to marry a princess – but only a true princess would do. In order to find her, he travelled far and wide, all over the land.

He met young princesses and old ones, beautiful princesses and plain ones, rich princesses and poor ones, but there was always something that was not quite right with each of them.

The prince began to despair. He called together his courtiers and announced, "I have failed to find my dream princess. We will go home to our palace without delay."

One dark night, back at his palace, there was the most tremendous storm. Lightning flashed across the sky and thunder buffeted the thick palace walls.

The prince and his parents were talking in the drawing room. He was telling them all about his hopeless search for a perfect princess to marry.

"Don't despair, my dear," said his mother, the queen. "Who knows what surprises the future holds. You could find your perfect princess just when you least expect to."

Suddenly, they heard a tiny tap-tapping at the window.

The prince opened it, and standing there before him was a very beautiful, but very wet, young lady. Her hair was dripping, her dress was soaked through, and she was shivering with cold.

"I am a princess," she told the prince, "and I am lost. Please may I come in and take shelter from the storm?"

The prince was astonished. He asked the girl into the palace, then he turned to the queen and whispered in her ear, "Oh, Mother, she is enchanting! But how can I be sure she really is a princess?"

"Leave it to me," said his mother, and she hurried off to have a bedroom prepared for the pretty girl.

First, the queen placed a little green pea on the mattress. Then she ordered the servants to bring twenty thick mattresses, and twenty feather quilts, which they piled on top of the pea. The princess needed a very tall ladder to climb into bed that night!

The next morning, at breakfast, the queen asked the princess if she had slept well.

"I had the most awful night!" said the princess. "I don't know what it was, but there was a hard lump under my bed, and it kept me awake all night, and now I'm absolutely covered with bruises!"

"At last!" the queen exclaimed, "our search is over! We have found a true princess for our son. Only a real princess would have skin so tender and delicate that she could feel a pea through a bed made from twenty mattresses and twenty feather quilts!"

Of course, the prince was overjoyed, he had found a true princess just when he was giving up hope!

Much to the delight of everyone, the prince and the princess were soon married in the castle chapel.

As for the little green pea, the prince had a cabinet made and it was put on display in the royal museum, where it can still be seen today!

# There's
# No Room
# Here

It was a very hot day down on Apple Tree Farm. The chicks trotted off to sit in the cool barn – but the cows had got there first!

"There's no room in here for you chicks!" mooed Mrs Cow. "Try the duck pond." But the duck pond was full of splashing ducks!

"This is not a chick pond!" quacked Mrs Duck. So, the chicks waddled past the pigsty, where Mr Pig was rolling in a big, squidgy mudbath.

"That looks very cool," called the chicks, peeping round the fence.

"Yes!" grunted the greedy pig. "And it's all for me!"

Then Robbie Chick had an idea. "Follow me!" he cried. As the three hot chicks followed him into the farmer's garden a fountain of water shot up in the air and splashed all the chicks! "It feels great!" giggled Rosie.

The little chicks ran in and out of the cool water all afternoon until it was time for tea. On the way home, they saw that the sun had dried up Mr Pig's mudbath. The ducks had splashed all the water out of the pond, and the cows were moaning in the hot milking parlour. But the very cool chicks just chuckled and dripped their way back home to Mummy.

# The Great Egg Hunt

On Sunnybrook Farm, there lived a very forgetful hen called Hetty. One day Hetty couldn't remember where she had laid her eggs. She searched the farmyard. "Oh, where did I put my babies?" she cried.

"Don't worry," quacked Dolly, kindly. She waddled off to get the other farm animals – the Great Egg Hunt had begun!

Jake the sheep found one egg amongst the brambles, Gus the goat found one on top of a cabbage leaf in the compost heap! Harry the horse found one in a rabbit hole, Claudia the cow found another in a clump of hay!

"But there's still one missing! I laid five eggs!" squawked Hetty. Then, Penny the pig spotted the last one nestling under a very old wheelbarrow.

"Hooray!" shouted the other animals in delight. Sam the sheepdog scooped all the eggs on to an old sack and carried them to the hen house. "Oh, thank you, thank you!" clucked Hetty the hen, as she settled herself on top of the five eggs.

The next morning, one by one, five, fat, fluffy chicks hatched out! Hetty proudly took the baby chicks out of the hen house, to show the other farm animals – a very happy ending to their Great Egg Hunt.

# The Tale of Two Princesses

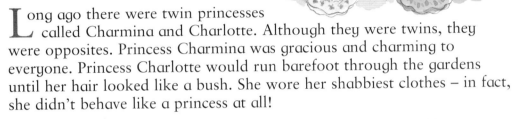

Long ago there were twin princesses called Charmina and Charlotte. Although they were twins, they were opposites. Princess Charmina was gracious and charming to everyone. Princess Charlotte would run barefoot through the gardens until her hair looked like a bush. She wore her shabbiest clothes – in fact, she didn't behave like a princess at all!

One day there was to be a ball at the palace. The guests of honour were two princes from the next kingdom. The two princesses, dressed in their new ball gowns, kept getting in the way of the preparations. "Why don't you go for a walk until our guests arrive," suggested the queen. "But stay together, don't get dirty and don't be late!"

The two princesses walked to the bottom of the palace gardens. "Let's go into the forest," said Princess Charlotte.

"I think we should go back," Princess Charmina told her sister. "We'll be late for the ball." But Princess Charlotte persuaded her to go a little further, so they set off again going even deeper into the forest. Finally, they came upon two horses in a clearing, but there was no sign of their riders. Just then they heard voices calling out, "Who's there?"

At first, the two princesses couldn't see where the voices were coming from. In the middle of the clearing there was a large pit. They peered over the edge. Princess Charmina stared in astonishment. Princess Charlotte burst out laughing. There at the bottom of the pit were two princes.

"Well don't just stand there," said the princes. "Help us out!"

The two princesses found ropes and threw one end down to the princes. They tied the other end to the horses. Soon the princes were rescued.

On their return they found the king and queen furious that their daughters had returned late looking so dirty. But their anger turned to joy when the two princes explained what had happened.

Everyone enjoyed the ball. The two princesses danced all night with the two princes. From that time on, Charlotte paid more attention to her gowns and hair. And Charmina became a little more playful and daring than before!

# The Three Little Pigs

Once upon a time, there were three little pigs who lived with their mummy in a big stone house.

One day, Mummy Pig said, "Children, it's time for you to go out and find your fortune in the big wide world." So she packed a little bag of food and a drink for each of them, and sent them on their way.

"Goodbye!" she called, as the three little pigs set off on their adventure. "Good luck, my dears, and remember to watch out for the big, bad wolf!"

"We will, Mummy," called the little pigs as they waved goodbye.

After a while, the three little pigs stopped for a rest and decided that they should each build a house to live in. Just then, they saw a farmer coming along the road with a wagon full of golden straw.

"Please, sir," said the first little pig, "may I have some of your straw to build myself a house?"

"Yes, little pig," said the farmer, "of course you can."

So the first little pig built his house of straw. Soon it was finished. It looked very good indeed, and the first little pig was happy.

The other two little pigs set off on their journey together and, after a while, they met a man carrying a large bundle of sticks.

"Please, sir," said the second little pig, "may I have some of your sticks to build myself a house?"

"Yes, little pig," said the man, "of course you can."

So the second little pig built his house of sticks. Soon it was finished. It looked very good indeed, and the second little pig was happy.

The third little pig set off on his journey alone. He saw lots of people with wagons of straw and bundles of sticks, but he did not stop until he met a man with a cart filled to the brim with bricks.

"Please, sir," said the third little pig, "may I have some bricks so that I can build myself a house?"

"Yes, little pig," said the man, "of course you can."

So the third little pig built his house of bricks. Soon it was finished. It looked very good indeed. It was strong and solid, and the third little pig was very, very pleased.

That evening, the big, bad wolf was walking along the road. He was very hungry and looking for something good to eat. He saw the first little pig's house of straw and looked in through the window.

"Yum, yum," he said to himself, licking his lips. "This little pig would make a most tasty dinner."

So, in his friendliest voice, the wolf called through the window, "Little pig, little pig, please let me in!"

But the first little pig remembered his mummy's warning, so he replied, "No, no, I won't let you in, not by the hair on my chinny-chin-chin!"

This made the wolf really angry. "Very well!" he roared. "I'll huff and I'll puff, and I'll blow your house down!"

The poor little pig was very afraid, but he still would not let the wolf in. So the wolf huffed... and he puffed... and he BLEW the straw house down.

Then the big, bad wolf chased the little pig and gobbled him up!

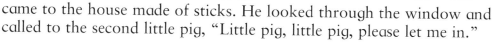

But the wolf was still hungry! He walked down the road and soon came to the house made of sticks. He looked through the window and called to the second little pig, "Little pig, little pig, please let me in."

"No, no!" cried the second little pig. "I won't let you in, not by the hair on my chinny-chin-chin!"

"Very well," cried the wolf. "Then I'll huff and I'll puff, and I'll blow your house down!"

And that's just what the big, bad wolf did. He huffed... and he puffed... and he BLEW the stick house down! Then he gobbled up the second little pig.

But the big, bad wolf was still hungry. So he walked down the road and soon came to the house made of bricks.

He looked through the window and called to the third little pig, "Little pig, little pig, please let me in."

"No, no!" cried the third little pig. "I won't let you in, not by the hair on my chinny-chin-chin!"

"Very well," roared the big, bad wolf. "I'll huff and I'll puff, and I'll blow your house down!"

So the wolf huffed and he puffed… he HUFFED and he PUFFED… and he HUFFED and he PUFFED some more, but he could not blow the brick house down!

By now the big, bad wolf was very, very angry. He scrambled up onto the roof and began to climb down through the chimney.

But the third little pig was a clever little pig, and he had put a big pot of boiling water to bubble on the fire.

When the wolf came down the chimney, he landed – ker-splosh! – right in the middle of the pot of boiling water! He burned his bottom so badly that he ran out of the house and down the road just as fast as his legs could carry him, howling so loudly with pain that he could be heard for miles.

The third little pig was very pleased with his house of bricks and lived in it for many years, happy and content. And nothing was ever heard of the big, bad wolf again.

# The Naughty Mermaids

Of all the mermaids that lived in the sea, Jazz and Cassandra were the naughtiest. They were not supposed to swim above sea when there were people about. But their latest prank was to swim to the lighthouse and call out to the little boy, Jack, who lived there.

"Coo-ee," they would call and, when the little boy looked towards them, they giggled and dived under the waves. When King Neptune heard about it, he was very cross indeed!

One day, Jack's mum made him a picnic. Jack laid the food on a cloth on the rocks. He had pizza and crisps and fizzy drink and chocolate. The two naughty mermaids popped up from the waves and saw all the food.

"Hello!" they called to Jack. "Are you going to eat all this food by yourself?" Jack was surprised, he'd never seen a mermaid.

"Yes," said Jack. "I mean, no! You can have some of my picnic, if you like." The mermaids had never had pizza or fizzy drink or chocolate, and they ate until they felt sick! They swam home, hoping King Neptune wouldn't spot them. But he did, and he called them to see him.

"Be warned!" said King Neptune. "Mermaids are not like children. They cannot behave like children and they cannot eat the food that children eat!"

For a while Jazz and Cassandra ate shrimps and seaweed, but they soon became bored and longed for some pizza. So the naughty mermaids swam up to the surface.

Jack was there with another picnic. The mermaids ate everything, then they played hide and seek in the waves with Jack. But, oh dear! When the mermaids tried to swim back to the bottom of the sea, their tails had become stiff and heavy! King Neptune was right. Mermaids can't behave like children.

Jack knew exactly what to do! He got his net and bucket and collected shrimps and seaweed from the rock pools. For three days and three nights he fed the mermaids proper mermaid food. By the third day they could move their tails again and swim.

When they arrived home King Neptune was waiting for them. This time, King Neptune wasn't angry – he was glad to see them back safely. "I hope you have learned a lesson," he said, quite gently. "Jack has been a good friend so you can play with him again. As long as you don't eat his food!"

# The Red Daffodil

It was spring time and all the daffodils were pushing their heads up towards the warmth of the sun. Slowly, their golden petals unfolded to let their yellow trumpets dance in the breeze. One particular field of daffodils was a blaze of gold like all the others – but right in the middle was a single splash of red. For there in the middle was a red daffodil.

From the moment she opened her petals, the red daffodil knew she was different from the other flowers. They sneered at her and whispered to each other. "What a strange, poor creature!" said one.

"She must envy our beautiful golden colour," said another.

Indeed it was true. The red daffodil wished very much that she was like the others. Instead of being proud of her red petals, she was ashamed and hung her head low. "What's wrong with me?" she thought. "Why aren't there any other red daffodils in the field?"

Passers-by stopped to admire the field of beautiful daffodils. "What a wonderful sight!" they exclaimed. And the daffodils' heads swelled with pride and danced in the breeze all the more merrily.

Then someone spotted the red daffodil right in the middle of the field. "Look at that extraordinary flower!" the man shouted. Everyone peered into the centre of the field.

"You're right," said someone else, "there's a red daffodil in the middle." Soon a large crowd had gathered, all pointing and laughing at the red daffodil.

She could feel herself blushing even redder at the attention. "How I wish my petals would close up again," she said to herself in anguish. But try as she might, her fine red trumpet stood out for all to see.

Now, in the crowd of people gathered at the edge of the field was a little girl. People were pushing and shoving and she couldn't see anything

at all. At last, her father lifted her high upon his shoulders so that she could see into the field.

"Oh!" exclaimed the little girl in a very big voice. "So that's the red daffodil. I think it's really beautiful. What a lucky daffodil to be so different."

And do you know, other people heard what the little girl said and they began to whisper to each other, "Well, I must say, I actually thought myself it was rather pretty, you know." Before long, people were praising the daffodil's beauty and saying it must be a very special flower. The red daffodil heard what the crowd was saying. Now she was blushing with pride and held her head as high as all the other daffodils in the field.

The other daffodils were furious. "What a foolish crowd," said one indignantly. "We are the beautiful ones!" They turned their heads away from the red daffodil and ignored her. She began to feel unhappy again.

By now word had spread far and wide about the amazing red daffodil and people came from all over the land to see her. Soon, the king's daughter got to hear about the red daffodil. "I must see this for myself," said the princess. She set off with her servant and eventually they came to the field where the red daffodil grew. When the princess saw her, she clapped her hands with glee.

"The red daffodil is more beautiful than I ever imagined," she cried. Then she had an idea. "Please bring my pet dove," she said to her servant. The man looked rather puzzled, but soon he returned with the bird. "As you know," said the princess to the servant, "I am to be married tomorrow and I would dearly love to have that red daffodil in my wedding bouquet."

The princess sent the dove into the middle of the field and it gently picked up the daffodil in its beak and brought her back to where the princess stood. The princess carried the daffodil back to the palace. She put the daffodil in a vase of water and there she stayed until the next day.

In the morning, the princess's servant took the red daffodil to the church. She could hear the bells and see all the guests assembling for the wedding ceremony. Then she saw the princess arrive in a coach driven by four white horses. How lovely the princess looked in her white gown and her head crowned with deep red roses.

As the servant reached the church door, the princess's lady-in-waiting stepped forward holding a huge bouquet of flowers into which she placed the red daffodil just as the flowers were handed to the princess. For a while, the red daffodil was overcome by the powerful scents of the other flowers in the bouquet, but when at last she looked around her she realised, with astonishment, that all of them were red. There were red daisies, red lilies, red carnations and red foxgloves. "Welcome," said one of the daisies, "you're one of us." And for the first time in her life, the red daffodil felt really at home.

After the wedding, the princess scattered the flowers from her bouquet among the flowers in her garden. Every spring, when she opened her petals, the red daffodil found she was surrounded by lots of other red flowers, and she lived happily in the garden for many, many years.

# You Can Do It, Dilly Duck!

It was the night before Dilly's first swimming lesson. "I've got a funny feeling in my tummy," said Dilly, as Mamma Duck kissed her goodnight.

"Don't worry!" replied her mother. "Just close your eyes tightly and you'll soon fall asleep." Dilly shut her eyes and tried to go to sleep. But all she could think about was the lesson.

"What if I sink?" she worried. Dilly pictured Mamma Duck's smiling face. "If Mamma Duck can float, perhaps I can, too," she thought. Then she snuggled down to go to sleep.

Suddenly Dilly opened her eyes. "But I'll get all wet!" she quacked, shaking her feathers. Dilly thought about her friend Webster the frog. "Webster loves getting wet," she remembered. "He says it's fun!"

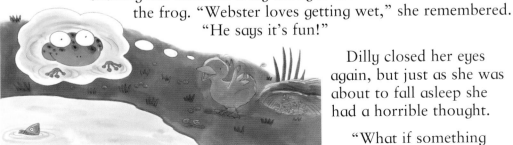

Dilly closed her eyes again, but just as she was about to fall asleep she had a horrible thought.

"What if something

nibbles my toes?" Dilly pictured all the bigger ducks doing duck-dives in the pond. "They're not afraid of what's under the water," she quacked, "so why should I be?"

Dilly was wide awake early the next morning, and so were all her friends.

"You can do it, Dilly!" they cheered as she waddled slowly to the edge of the pond. She leaned forward and looked in, very timidly. There in the water was another little duckling gazing back at her. Dilly looked at the other little duckling. She was small and yellow with downy feathers, just like Dilly.

"Well, if you can do it, I guess I can too!"quacked Dilly bravely. SPLASH! She jumped right into the pond. "I can float!" cried Dilly, paddling along. "It's fun getting wet!" Then Dilly did a duck-dive.

"There's nothing scary under the water either!" she added, bobbing up again. "In fact, you are all right! I CAN do it!"

# Rumpelstiltskin

Once upon a time there was a boastful miller. One day, he told the king that his daughter was so clever that she could spin gold out of ordinary straw.

"I must meet this remarkable girl," said the king. "Bring her to the palace at once."

The king took the miller's daughter to a room filled with straw. In one corner stood a spinning wheel. "You must spin all this straw into gold before morning," the king told the girl, "or you will be put to death." Then he went out and locked the door behind him.

The poor girl sat at the spinning wheel and wept. However could she make gold from straw? Suddenly, the door flew open, and in leapt a funny-looking little man.

"Why are you crying?" he asked.

When the girl told him what the king had said, the strange man replied,

"What will you give me if I spin this straw into gold for you?"

"My pearl necklace," said the girl.

So the little man sat down at the spinning wheel and quickly spun all the straw into gold. Then he magically vanished from the room.

The next morning, the king was amazed – but now he wanted even more gold. He took the girl to an even bigger room full of straw. Again he told her to spin the straw into gold by morning, or she would die, and then left.

The poor girl sat down and wept. Suddenly, the odd little man appeared. "What will you give me if I help you this time?" he asked.

"My pretty ring," the girl replied.

So the little man began to spin, and soon all the straw had been turned into gold. Then he vanished.

The next morning the greedy king was astounded but still not satisfied. He took the girl to an even bigger room, piled to the ceiling with straw. "If you succeed this time, you will become queen," the king said. "If you fail, you know what will happen."

As soon as the girl was alone, the little man appeared. "I have nothing left to give you," said the girl.

"Then you must promise me your first-born child when you are queen," said the man.

The girl thought she might never be queen and have a child, and so she

agreed. The strange little man sat at the spinning wheel and began to work. He spun for many hours and the pile of gold grew and grew.

"At last," said the little man, "my task is done." Then he vanished. The room was piled from floor to ceiling with stacks of glistening gold that shone like the sun.

At dawn, the king was overjoyed. He kept his promise and soon married the miller's daughter.

A year later, the king and queen had a baby. The queen had forgotten all about her promise –

but the funny little man had not. He appeared in the queen's bedchamber. "I have come for your baby!" he announced.

"I will give you gold, anything you wish, but don't take my baby," cried the queen. She wept so much that the little man was sorry for her.

"Very well," he said. "If you can guess my name within three nights you may keep your baby. If not, the child is mine!" Then he disappeared.

The queen sent messengers out to collect names from all over the kingdom. They returned with their suggestions. The next two evenings, when the little man arrived, the queen questioned him again and again:

"Is your name Tom? Jack? Dick? Peter?" she asked, but the strange man shook his head. "Brutus then?"

Each time, the reply was the same: "No, Your Majesty."

By the third day, one messenger had not returned. That afternoon, on his way back to the palace, he saw a hut in a forest clearing. In front of it, an odd little man was dancing around a fire, singing:

*"I'll be the winner of this game!
The queen will never guess my name!
She will lose, and I will win,
Because my name is…
Rumpelstiltskin!"*

The messenger galloped back to the palace and told the queen what he had seen and heard. She was so grateful that she rewarded the messenger with a huge sack of gold.

That night, the queen eagerly waited in her throne room for the little man. When he appeared, the queen asked, "Is your name Guzzletum?"

"No, no, it's not!" laughed the little man.

"Is it Bumblebottom? Is it Jigglejoggle? Is it Tickletooth or Wigglewoggle?"

"No! No!" he cackled. "Your time's running out, Your Majesty!"

The queen smiled. "Could it be... Rumpelstiltskin?"

The little man could not believe his ears and flew into a rage. "Who told you? Who told you?" he shrieked. "How did you find out?"

He cried and squealed. He stamped his feet and beat the floor with his fists. "You've won! You've won!" he wailed, and disappeared in a shower of sparks.

The little man never came back to worry the queen, and they all lived happily ever after.

# Boink!

Boink was a small round monster. His name was Boink, but it was also the sound he made when he moved around. You and I can walk and run, but Boink the monster bounced like a ball – BOINK! BOINK! BOINK! – until he got to where he was going. He looked like a space hopper toy and he was rubbery too, to help him bounce.

No one knew that Boink lived in an empty dog kennel at the end of Joe's garden. He only had one problem, he had nothing to play with.

Joe didn't have anyone to play with but he had lots of toys. Boink watched him as played with his cars. As Joe played he made a strange sound. "Brmmm!" he went, "Brmmm! Brmmm!"

Boink practised making the noise on his own at night. "Brmmm!" he said softly, and then louder, "Brmmm! Brmmm!" But it wasn't any fun without the cars. Boink wanted some toys of his own. So he decided to borrow some!

One night, when Joe was asleep, Boink bounced in through Joe's open window. In the bedroom there were toys everywhere. Boink took two cars out of the toy box. Then he bounced back out of the window.

The first thing Joe noticed in the morning was that some of his cars were missing. But Joe soon forgot the cars and played with his aeroplanes. "Neeaw! Neeaw!" he shouted as he ran round the garden. Boink watched Joe playing, and that night he took two aeroplanes from Joe's bedroom!

Joe's mum said he must have left them in the garden, but Joe knew he hadn't. Joe had to play with his train set instead.

That night Joe pretended to go to sleep. He couldn't believe his eyes when he saw a roly poly monster bounce in through the window and take his train set! As Boink bounced back out of the window Joe leapt out of bed and watched him disappear with the train set into the kennel.

After breakfast, Joe went to the dog kennel and peeped inside. There, fast asleep, was the roly poly monster. All around him were Joe's missing toys! Joe was so surprised, he gave a startled yelp and Boink woke up.

"Let's play with the train set," said Joe. "Toot! Toot!" said Boink. And that's what they did. When Joe's mum looked out of the window, she was pleased to see that Joe had found his missing toys. And she was surprised to see a space hopper in the garden!

"You can play with me if you like," said Joe, "but you must promise never to take my toys without asking."

# The Castle in the Clouds

There was once a family that lived in a little house in a village at the bottom of a mountain. At the top of the mountain was a great, grey castle made of granite. The castle was always shrouded in clouds, so it was known as the castle in the clouds. From the village you could only just see the outline of its high walls and turrets. No one in the village ever went near the castle, for it looked such a gloomy and forbidding place.

Now in this family there were seven children. One by one they went out into the world to seek their fortune, and at last it was the youngest child's turn. His name was Sam. His only possession was a pet cat named Jess, and she was an excellent rat-catcher. Sam was most upset at the thought of leaving Jess behind when he went off to find work, but then he had an idea. "I'll offer Jess's services at the castle in the clouds. They're bound to need a good ratter, and I'm sure I can find work there, too," he thought.

His parents were dismayed to discover that Sam intended to seek work at the castle, but try as they might they could not change his mind. So Sam set off for the castle with Jess at his side. Soon the road started to wind up the mountainside through thick pine forests. It grew cold and misty. Rounding a bend they suddenly found themselves up against a massive, grey stone wall. They followed the curve of the wall until they came to the castle door.

Sam went up to the door and banged on it. The sound echoed spookily. "Who goes there?" said a voice.

Looking up, Sam saw that a window high in the wall had been thrown open and a face was eyeing him suspiciously.

"I... I... I wondered if you'd be interested in employing my cat as a rat-catcher," began Sam.

The window slammed shut, but a moment later a hand beckoned him through the partly open castle door. Stepping inside, Sam and Jess found themselves face-to-face with an old man.

"Rat-catcher, did you say?" said the old man raising one eyebrow.

"Very well, but she'd better do a good job or my master will punish us all!"

Sam sent Jess off to prove her worth. In the meantime Sam asked the old man, who was the castle guard, if there might be any work for him.

"You can help out in the kitchens, but it's hard work!" the guard said.

Sam was soon at work in the kitchens – and what hard work it was! He spent all day peeling vegetables, cleaning pans and scrubbing the floor. By midnight he was exhausted. He was about to find a patch of straw to make his bed, when he noticed Jess wasn't around, so he set off in search of her. Down dark passages he went, up winding staircases, but there was no sign of her. He was wondering how he would ever find his way back to the kitchens, when he caught sight of Jess's green eyes shining like lanterns at the top of a rickety spiral staircase. "Here, Jess!" called Sam softly. But Jess stayed just where she was.

When he reached her, he found that she was sitting outside a door and seemed to be listening to something on the other side. Sam put his ear to the door. He could hear the sound of sobbing. He knocked gently at the door. "Who is it?" said a girl's voice.

"I'm Sam, the kitchen boy. What's the matter? Can I come in?" said Sam.

"If only you could," sobbed the voice. "I'm Princess Rose. When my father died my uncle locked me in here and stole the castle. Now I fear I shall never escape!"

Sam pushed and pushed at the door, but to no avail. "Don't worry," he said, "I'll get you out of here."

Sam knew exactly what to do, for when he had been talking to the guard, he had spotted a pair of keys hanging on a nail in the rafters high above the old man's head. He had wondered at the time why anyone should put keys out of the reach of any human hand. Now he thought he knew – but first he had to get the keys himself!

Sam and Jess finally made their way back to where the keys were, only to find the guard was fast asleep in his chair right underneath them! Quick as a flash, Jess had leaped up on to the shelf behind his head. From there, she climbed higher and higher until she reached the rafters. She carefully took the keys in her jaws and began to carry them gingerly down.

But as she jumped from the shelf again, Jess knocked over a jug and sent it crashing to the floor. The guard woke with a start. "Who goes there?" he growled. He just caught sight of the tip of Jess's tail as she made a dash for the door.

Sam and Jess retraced their steps with the guard in hot pursuit. "You go a different way," hissed Sam, running up the stairs to Rose's door, while the old man disappeared off after Jess. Sam put one of the keys in the lock. It fitted! He turned the key and opened the door. There stood the loveliest girl he had ever seen. The princess ran towards him, as he cried, "Quick! There's not a moment to lose." He grabbed her hand and led her out of the tower.

"Give me the keys," she said. She led him down to the castle cellars. At last they came to a tiny door. The princess put the second key in the lock and the door opened. Inside was a small cupboard, and inside that was a beautiful casket filled with precious jewels.

"My own casket – and all my jewels! My uncle stole these from me!" cried Rose.

Grabbing the casket the pair ran to the stables and saddled a horse. Suddenly Jess appeared with the guard still chasing her. With a mighty leap Jess landed on the back of the horse behind the princess and Sam. "Off we go!" cried Sam.

And that was the last that any of them saw of the castle in the clouds. Sam married the princess and they all lived happily ever after.

# The Yellow Bluebells

The garden at Corner Cottage was full of flowers and it was the fairies' job to look after them. They were never seen because they worked at night. Blossom, the youngest fairy, was also one of the busiest. It was her job to paint all the bluebells which spread out under the apple tree like a deep, blue carpet.

One evening, Blossom was sick. "I've got a terrible cold," she told her friend Petal, sniffing loudly. "I can't work tonight."

"I wish I could help," said Petal, "but I've got to spray the flowers with perfume or they won't smell right. You'll have to ask the gnomes."

All the gnomes really liked doing was fishing and playing tricks. "No problem!" said Chip and Chuck when she asked them. "Just leave it to us." But when Blossom got up the next morning the gnomes had painted some of the bluebells… YELLOW! She couldn't believe it.

"Have you seen what they've done?" she said to Petal. "What will Jamie think?" Jamie lived in Corner Cottage with his mum and dad.

When he went into the garden he sat on his favourite branch of the apple tree  and looked down. "I'm sure those flowers were blue," he thought and decided to pick some for his mother.

"Yellowbells?" said Mum, putting them into a jam jar. "I don't remember planting those."

That night, Blossom was still feeling ill. "You'll have to paint the yellowbells," she told the gnomes. Chip and Chuck just chuckled and in the morning Jamie found that the flowers were PINK! He picked some for his mum to go with the yellowbells.

When Petal told Blossom, she groaned. "I just knew something like this would happen." But she was still feeling too sick to work.

"Don't worry," said Petal. "Leave it to me." And she made the naughty gnomes paint all the pinkbells again. And this time she watched them!

The next morning, all the bluebells were blue again, and Blossom was feeling much better. When Jamie and his mum went into the garden, everything was as it should be. The bluebells were the right colour. And there was no sign of the yellowbells or pinkbells.

"It must have been the fairies!" joked Mum.

"Maybe it really was the fairies," thought Jamie as he drifted off to sleep that night.

# A Spelling Lesson

Wanda Witch was wandering through a very spooky wood. She loved to practise spooky spells, and the thought of doing anything good made her feel really ill. She took great delight in turning a patch of beautiful bluebells into a pool of smelly, slimy goo. Then she gave a tree a creepy face that would frighten anyone who happened to be passing.

Creeping through the undergrowth, Wanda came upon a wizard, standing gazing into a pond. As quick as lightning, she waved her wand and the wizard fell straight into the water! Although the water wasn't very deep, it was very cold and full of horrible, slimy weeds.

The wizard leapt out in one huge jump, and was so angry with Wanda that he cast a spell as he jumped. His big red cloak wrapped itself around Wanda's body and began to squeeze her really tight.

"Say sorry!" roared the wizard.

Wanda was shocked to have met someone even speedier and nastier than her! Hastily, she apologised to the wizard, and promised that from now on there would be no more nasty spells!

# Witch's Brew

**W**innie Witch was having a wonderful time! She was in her kitchen, deep inside a dark cave, stirring a huge cauldron. She was singing the spell for a magic monster as she threw the ingredients into the pot. They had taken her days to collect. Eye of lizard, toe of frog, tail of rat and bark of dog, sneeze of chicken, lick of weasel and smell of cat were easy – but the cough of bat had been hard. It whizzed through the night sky really fast but eventually the bat must have choked on a fly. With a cough and a splutter, it slowed down enough for Winnie to scoop up a cough. Then she flew home on her broomstick for a rest!

The cauldron began to bubble furiously as Winnie stirred faster. Then... a monster's head began rising out of the pot.

"Ah!" sighed Winnie, "very pleased to meet you!"

"Mmm! Very pleased to *eat* you!" replied the monster!

This wasn't right! Winnie grabbed her wand and shook it at the monster, whispering a spell. With a whoosh and a bang, the monster vanished. Winnie won't try that spell again!

# The
# Disappearing Trick

Like all little kittens, Smoky was very playful. One day, she was chasing her ball, when it rolled under the fence into the garden next door. Forgetting about the mean dog who lived there, Smoky squeezed through the fence, just in time to see her ball disappear into a hole in the grass...

Smoky looked down into the hole, but it was very deep and there was no sign of the ball. Just then, she heard a low growl, and turned to see an angry dog snarling at her.

In a flash, she scrambled into the hole, with the dog's sharp teeth snapping at her heels. She squeezed down a long tunnel and into a little room at the bottom.

"Hello!" said Rabbit, handing Smoky the ball. "Have you lost this?"

Smoky was amazed to find she was in Rabbit's burrow. She told him about the angry dog. "Don't worry," said Rabbit, "we'll trick him!"

He dug a new tunnel and in no time they were back in Smoky's garden.

"Over here!" Rabbit called through the fence to the dog, still guarding the hole! How the two friends laughed to see the puzzled look on his face.

# Jack and the Beanstalk

Jack was a lively young boy who lived with his mother in a tiny little cottage in the country.

Jack and his mother were very poor. They had straw on the floor, and many panes of glass in their windows were broken. The only thing of value that was left was a cow.

One day, Jack's mother called him in from the garden, where he was chopping logs for their stove. "You will have to take Daisy the cow to market and sell her," she said sadly.

As Jack trudged along the road to market, he met a strange old man.

"Where are you taking that fine milking cow?" asked the man.

"To market, sir," replied Jack, "to sell her."

"If you sell her to me," said the man, "I will give you these beans. They are special, magic beans. I promise you won't regret it."

When Jack heard the word "magic", he became very excited. He quickly swapped the cow for the beans, and ran all the way home.

Jack rushed through the cottage door. "Mother! Mother!" he called. "Where are you?"

"Why are you home so soon?" asked Jack's mother, coming down the stairs. "How much did you get for the cow?"

"I got these," said Jack, holding out his hand. "They're magic beans!"

"What?" shrieked his mother. "You sold our only cow for a handful of beans? You silly boy, come here!"

Angrily, she snatched the beans from Jack's hand and flung them out of the window and into the garden. Jack was sent to bed with no supper that night.

The next morning, Jack's rumbling stomach woke him early. His room was strangely dark. As he got dressed, he glanced out of his window – and what he saw took his breath away.

Overnight, a beanstalk had sprung up in the garden. Its trunk was almost as thick as Jack's cottage and its top was so tall that it disappeared into the clouds.

Jack yelled with excitement and rushed outside. As he began to climb the beanstalk, his mother stood at the bottom and begged for him to come back down, but he took no notice.

At last, tired and very hungry, Jack reached the top. He found himself in a strange land full of clouds. He could see something glinting in the distance and began walking towards it. Eventually he reached the biggest castle he had ever seen. Maybe he could find some food there?

He crept under the front door and ran straight into an enormous foot!

"What was that?" boomed a female voice, and the room shook. Jack found himself looking into a huge eye, then he was whisked into the air by a giant hand!

"And who are you?" roared the voice.

"I'm Jack," said Jack, "and I'm tired and hungry. Please can you give me something to eat and a place to rest for a while?"

The giant woman was a kind old lady and took pity on the tiny boy. "Don't make a sound," she whispered. "My husband doesn't like boys and will eat you if he finds you." Then she gave Jack a crumb of warm bread and a thimble full of hot soup.

He was drinking the last drop when the woman said, "In the cupboard, quickly! My husband's here!"

From inside the dark cupboard, Jack could hear the approach of thundering footsteps. Then a deep voice bellowed, "Fee, fie, foe, fum, I smell the blood of an Englishman! Be he alive or be he dead, I'll grind his bones to make my bread!"

Jack peeped out through a knothole in the cupboard door, and saw a huge giant standing beside the table.

"Wife!" shouted the giant. "I can smell a boy in the house!"

"Nonsense, my dear," said the giant's wife soothingly. "All you can smell is this lovely dinner that I have made for you. Now, do sit down and eat."

When the giant had gobbled up his huge dinner, he shouted, "Wife! Bring me my gold – now! I wish to count it!"

Jack saw the giant's wife bring out several enormous sacks of coins. The giant picked one up and a cascade of gold fell onto the table top.

Then Jack watched the giant count the coins, one by one. The giant began to stack them up in piles as he worked.

After a while, he started to yawn, and, not long after, Jack saw that he had fallen asleep. Soon Jack heard very loud snoring!

"It's time I made a move!" Jack said to himself. And, quick as a flash, he leapt out of the cupboard, grabbed a sack of gold, slid down the table leg and ran for the door.

But the giant's wife heard him. "Stop, thief!" she screamed at the top of her voice, which woke her husband. He jumped up in a hurry and ran after Jack, shouting loudly, "Come back!"

Jack ran until he came to the top of the beanstalk. Then, with the giant still after him, he scrambled down as fast as he could.

"Mother!" he called, as he got closer to the ground. "Mother, get the axe, quickly!"

By the time Jack reached the bottom, his mother was there with the axe. She chopped down the beanstalk, and the giant came crashing down with it – he never got up again!

Now that they had the gold, Jack and his mother were very rich. They wouldn't have to worry about anything ever again and they lived happily ever after.

# The Princess who Never Smiled

A long time ago, in a far off land, a princess was born. The king and queen called her Princess Columbine. They thought she was the most precious child ever to be born. And, to make sure that she was watched over every minute of every day, they hired a nurse to look after her.

One day the queen came to the nursery and found the nurse asleep and the little princess crying. The queen was very cross and called for the king who told off the nurse for not watching the baby. But what the king and queen didn't know was that the nurse was really a wicked enchantress, and she cast a spell over the baby princess: "Princess Columbine will not smile again until she learns my real name!"

And from that day on, the princess never smiled! The king and queen tried names from all over the land, unusual names and even outlandish names such as Dorominty, Truditta, Charlottamina. But none broke the spell.

Princess Columbine grew up to be a sweet and beautiful girl. But her face was always sad. The king and queen tried everything to make her smile. They bought her a puppy. They even hired a court jester who told the silliest jokes.

"Why did the ice cream?" asked the jolly jester. The princess shrugged.

"Because the jelly wobbled!" the jester guffawed, but the princess just gazed at him politely. The jester soon gave up.

One day an artist called Rudolpho asked if he could paint the princess's portrait. The king agreed, but only if he painted the princess smiling. Rudolpho set up his easel beneath a large mirror and began.

Soon the princess's portrait was complete, all except for her smile. Rudolpho tried some funny drawings to make the princess smile. Then he drew a picture of her old nurse with a moustache, and wrote NURSE.

Princess Columbine gazed at the picture in the mirror. There, underneath the picture, was the word NURSE spelled out back to front. "ESRUN," Princess Columbine said quietly. And then she smiled.

"Her name is ESRUN!" laughed Princess Columbine. At last the spell was broken! Everyone was so happy that soon they were all laughing too – but Princess Columbine laughed the loudest.

# Town Mouse and Country Mouse

Once there was a roly-poly, wiggly-whiskered mouse, who lived in a snug little nest under an oak tree. Country Mouse loved his home. He had plenty of acorns, nuts and berries to eat and a warm and cosy straw bed to sleep in. Squirrel and Robin, who lived in the oak tree, were the best neighbours he could ever wish for.

One day, Country Mouse had a surprise. His cousin, Town Mouse, came to visit from the Big City. Town Mouse was sleek and slender, with a smooth, shiny coat. His long whiskers were smart and elegant. Country Mouse felt a little ordinary beside him. But he didn't mind at all.

He just wanted to make Town Mouse feel welcome. "Are you hungry, Cousin?" he said. "Come and have some supper!"

But Town Mouse didn't like the acorns and blackberries that Country Mouse gave him to eat. They were tough and sour. And Town Mouse thought his cousin's friends were boring. The straw bed that he slept in that night was so rough and scratchy that he didn't sleep a wink!

Next day, Town Mouse said, "Come to the Big City with me, Cousin. It's so much more exciting than the country! I live in a grand house, eat delicious food and have exciting adventures. Come with me and see what you've been missing!" It sounded so wonderful, Country Mouse couldn't resist it so, saying goodbye to his friends, he set off for the city with his cousin.

When they arrived in the Big City, Country Mouse was frightened. It was so noisy – horns blared and wheels clattered all around them. Huge lorries roared and rumbled down the street and the smelly, smoky air made them choke and cough. And there were dogs everywhere!

At last, they arrived at Town Mouse's house. It was very grand, just as Town Mouse had said.

But it was so big! Country Mouse was afraid that he would get lost!

"Don't worry," said Town Mouse to Country Mouse. "You'll soon learn your way around the house. For now, just stay close to me. I'm starving – let's go and have a snack." Country Mouse was hungry, too, so he followed his cousin to the kitchen.

Country Mouse had never seen so much delicious food – there were plates full of fruit, nuts, cheese and cakes. He and his cousin ate and ate and ate! But Country Mouse wasn't used to this sort of rich food. Before he knew it, his tummy was aching.

Suddenly, a huge woman came into the room. "Eeek! Mice!" she screamed. She grabbed a big broom and began to swat the mice, who scampered off as fast as they could.

As the two mice scurried across the floor, Country Mouse thought things couldn't possibly get worse. But how wrong he was! A big cat suddenly sprang out from behind a chair! With a loud "MEEOOWW," he pounced on the two little mice. Country Mouse had never been so frightened. He darted and dashed as fast as his aching tummy would let him. The two mice jumped through a mousehole and were safe at last in Town Mouse's house.

"Phew! I think we've done enough for one day," said Town Mouse, when they had caught their breath. "Let's get some sleep," he said, with a stretch and a yawn.

"I'll show you the rest of the house in the morning." Country Mouse curled up in the hard little bed. But he was too frightened and unhappy to sleep. As he listened to his cousin snore, he tried hard not to cry.

Next morning, Town Mouse was ready for more adventures, but Country Mouse had had more than enough. "Thank you for inviting me," he told his cousin, "but I have seen all I want to see of the Big City. It is too big and noisy and dirty – and too full of danger for me. I want to go back to my quiet, peaceful home in the country."

So, Country Mouse went back to his snug, cosy home under the oak tree. He had never been so happy to see his friends – and they wanted to hear all about his adventures. Country Mouse was pleased to tell them everything that had happened in the Big City – but he never, ever went back there again!

# Easter Bunnies

It was Easter and the naughty bunnies had hidden eggs for the animals to find. How they chuckled when they saw the farm cat shaking water from her fur. She had been searching by the pond and had fallen in! The bunnies giggled as they watched the hens shooing the pig away from the henhouse. "They're not in here!" the hens clucked.

Eventually, when the animals had searched high and low, Daisy the cow said, "It's no use, we can't find them! We give up!"

"Here's a clue," said the bunnies. "Where do you find eggs?"

"In a nest," answered Mrs Goose.

"And what do you make a nest with?" asked the bunnies.

"Straw!" said the horse.

"They must be in the haystack!" cried all the animals at once.

They rushed to the field and there, hidden in the haystack, was a pile of lovely Easter eggs.

What a feast they had!

# Little Red Riding Hood

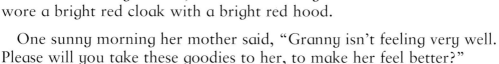

Once upon a time there was a little girl who lived with her mother at the edge of a deep, dark forest. Everyone called the girl "Little Red Riding Hood", because she always wore a bright red cloak with a bright red hood.

One sunny morning her mother said, "Granny isn't feeling very well. Please will you take these goodies to her, to make her feel better?"

"I will," replied Little Red Riding Hood.

"Remember," said her mother, "stay on the path, and don't stop to talk to any strangers on the way."

Little Red Riding Hood hopped and skipped along the path to Granny's house. She had only gone a short way into the deep, dark forest, when a sly, nasty wolf with big shiny teeth and long sharp claws jumped out onto the path, right in front of her.

"Hello, my pretty one," said the wolf. "Where are you going on this fine morning?"

"Good morning," said Little Red Riding Hood politely. "I'm going to see my granny, who isn't feeling very well. She lives all the way on the other side of the forest. But please excuse me, I am not allowed to talk to strangers."

"Of course, little girl," sneered the crafty wolf. "You must be in a hurry. But why not take a moment to pick a big bunch of these lovely wild flowers to cheer up your granny?"

"Thank you, Mr Wolf, that sounds like a very good idea," said Little Red Riding Hood, putting her basket down on the ground. "I'm sure that Granny would love them."

So, while Little Red Riding Hood picked a big bunch of sweet-smelling flowers, the wicked wolf raced ahead through the deep, dark forest and soon arrived at Granny's pretty cottage.

The wolf lifted the knocker and banged hard at the door.

Sweet old Granny sat up in bed. "Who is it?" she called.

"It's me, Little Red Riding Hood," replied the wolf in a voice which sounded just like Little Red Riding Hood's.

"Hello, my dear," called Granny. "The door is not locked – lift up the latch and come in."

So the wolf opened the door and, as quick as a flash, he gobbled up Granny. Then, he put on her nightie and nightcap, and crawled under the bedclothes to lie in wait for Little Red Riding Hood.

A short time later, Little Red Riding Hood arrived at the cottage and knocked on Granny's door.

"Who is it?" called the wolf, in a high voice sounding just like Granny.

"It's me, Granny," came the reply, "Little Red Riding Hood."

"Hello, my dear," called the wolf. "The door is not locked – lift up the latch and come in."

So Little Red Riding Hood lifted the latch, opened the door and went into Granny's cottage.

Little Red Riding Hood couldn't believe her eyes. "Oh, Granny," she said, "it is so nice to see you, but what big ears you have!"

"All the better to hear you with," said the wolf. "Come closer, my dear."

Little Red Riding Hood took a step closer to the bed.

"Oh, Granny," she said, "what big eyes you have!"

"All the better to see you with," said the wolf. "Come closer, my dear."

So Little Red Riding Hood took another step closer. Now she was right beside Granny's bed.

"Oh, Granny!" she cried. "What big teeth you have!"

"All the better to eat you with, my dear!" snarled the wolf, and he jumped up and swallowed Little Red Riding Hood in one BIG gulp!

Now it just so happened that a woodcutter was passing Granny's cottage that sunny morning. He was going to work on the other side of the forest. He knew that Granny had not been feeling very well, so he decided to look in on her.

What a surprise he had when he saw the hairy wolf fast asleep in Granny's bed!

When he saw the wolf's big, fat tummy, he knew just what had happened.

Quick as a flash, he took out his shiny, sharp axe and sliced the wolf open! Out popped Granny and Little Red Riding Hood, surprised and shaken, but safe and well.

The woodcutter dragged the wolf outside and threw him down a deep, dark well so he would never trouble anyone ever again. Then the woodcutter, Granny and Little Red Riding Hood sat down to tea and ate all of the yummy goodies from Little Red Riding Hood's basket.

After tea, Little Red Riding Hood waved goodbye to her Granny and the woodcutter and ran all the way home to her mother, without straying once from the path or talking to any strangers. What an eventful day!

# The Pig and the Jewels

Daisy was as pretty as a picture, and very kind too. Daisy looked after all the animals on the farm where she lived. She loved them all dearly, and the animals all loved her, too. But Daisy dreamt of being more than a farmer's daughter, she day-dreamed about being a princess.

One day she found a sick pig at the edge of the forest. She took him to the farm and nursed him back to health. The pig became her favourite animal, she told him all her secrets, and he listened carefully. She even told him the most important secret of all.

"Dear little pig," she whispered in his ear, "I wish, I wish I could be a princess!" That night the pig went away. When he returned the next morning, he had a tiara made of precious jewels on his head.

"Darling pig," cried Daisy, "is that for me?" Daisy put the tiara on her head. It fitted her perfectly.

The next night the pig went away and in the morning he returned with a beautiful necklace. Daisy put it on.

After that the pig went away every night for six

nights and returned with something different. First a dress of yellow silk, followed by a purple cloak and soft leather shoes. Then jewelled bracelets, and long lengths of satin ribbon for her hair. And, finally, a ring made of gold and rubies.

Daisy put on all the gifts the pig had brought her and stood in front of her mirror. "At last," she whispered, "I look just like a real princess."

The next day the pig disappeared again. Daisy didn't worry because she knew he always returned. But days went by and then weeks, and the pig did not return. Daisy missed him more than she could say.

One evening Daisy sat by the fire in her beautiful clothes. Suddenly there was a noise at the door. Opening it, she saw the pig!

With a cry of joy she bent to kiss him and, as she did, he turned into a handsome prince! Daisy gasped with amazement.

"Sweet Daisy," said the prince. "If it wasn't for you I would still be alone and friendless, wandering in the forest."

He explained how a wicked witch had cast a spell to turn him into a pig. "Your kiss broke the spell," said the prince. "Will you marry me, Daisy?" At long last, Daisy really was going to become Princess Daisy!

# Making a Splash!

One day, Mrs Hen and her chicks were walking near the pond, when Mrs Duck swam by, followed by a line of ducklings. The ducklings were playing games as they swam along. They chased each other around the pond and ducked down under the water.

"May we go in the water?" the chicks asked. "It looks like fun!"

"Oh, no, dears," said Mrs Hen. "Chicks and water don't mix! You haven't got the right feathers or feet!"

This made the chicks very miserable. "It's not fair!" they grumbled. "We wish we were ducklings!"

On the way home, a big black cloud appeared and it started to rain. Soon the chicks' fluffy feathers were wet through.

They scurried back to the henhouse as fast as they could and arrived wet, cold and shivering. They quickly snuggled under their mothers' wings and they were soon feeling better. Their feathers were dry and fluffy in no time at all.

"Imagine being wet all the time!" said the chicks. "Thank goodness we're not ducklings, after all!"

# The Enchanted Garden

The beautiful castle that Princess Sylvie grew up in had no garden, so she loved to walk through the meadows just to look at the flowers. One day Princess Sylvie found an old woman standing by an overgrown path. She asked the woman where the path led.

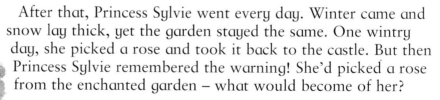

"To the garden of the enchantress!" replied the woman. "So be warned... don't pick the flowers!"

Princess Sylvie followed the path until she came to a small cottage with the prettiest garden she had ever seen!

After that, Princess Sylvie went every day. Winter came and snow lay thick, yet the garden stayed the same. One wintry day, she picked a rose and took it back to the castle. But then Princess Sylvie remembered the warning! She'd picked a rose from the enchanted garden – what would become of her?

But days passed and nothing happened. The rose stayed as fresh as the day it was picked. Then months passed and still nothing happened. Forgetting her fears, Princess Sylvie went back to the enchanted garden.

When she saw the garden, Princess Sylvie wanted to cry! The grass was brown, the flowers had withered and died. Then she heard someone weeping. The enchantress was by the fire in the cottage, crying. She was old and bent.

"What happened to your lovely garden?" the Princess asked.

"Someone picked a rose from my magic garden!" said the enchantress. "The picked flower will live forever, but the rest must die! When the rose was picked, my magic was lost! And now, I too will wither and die!"

"What can I do?" said Princess Sylvie, heartbroken.

"Only a princess can bring my magic back," she replied. "She must bring me six sacks of stinging nettles! No princess would do that!"

Princess Sylvie ran to the meadow. She gathered up six sacks of nettles, not caring that they stung her. She took them back to the enchantress.

"I am a princess, and here are the stinging nettles," said Princess Sylvie.

The enchantress made a potion with the nettles and drank it. Instantly, the garden became enchanted again! Gone was the bent old lady and in her place was a beautiful young woman.

"My beautiful garden is restored," smiled the enchantress, "and so am I!"

And so the two became great friends and shared the enchanted garden.

# Sleeping Beauty

Once upon a time, in a land far, far away, there lived a king and queen who were kind and good. When the queen gave birth to a baby girl, the whole kingdom rejoiced.

When it was time for the baby to be christened, the king and queen arranged a great celebration. They asked the seven good fairies of the kingdom to be the baby's godmothers. But, to their surprise, eight fairies arrived at the feast.

The eighth fairy was ugly and old, and no one had seen her for years. The king and queen, thinking she was dead, hadn't sent her an invitation to take part in the ceremony.

Soon it was time for the fairies to give the baby princess their magical presents. The first gave her the gift of beauty, the second gave her wisdom. The third fairy said she would be graceful, the fourth said that she would dance like the wind. The fifth and sixth gave her the gifts of music and song, so that she would sing and play like an angel.

Just before the seventh fairy stepped up to give the princess her gift, the eighth fairy pushed ahead of her. "The princess," she cackled, "will prick her finger on the spindle of a spinning wheel – and die!"

Everyone in the room was horrified, and the queen began to cry. But then the seventh fairy stepped forward. "Here is my gift," she said. "The princess will not die. Instead, when she pricks her finger, she will fall asleep for a hundred years. At the end of that time, a prince will come to wake her up."

The king and queen were relieved, but even so they ordered every spinning wheel in the kingdom to be destroyed. They couldn't bear to think of anything hurting their daughter.

The years passed and the princess grew into a lovely young girl, as wise, beautiful and graceful as the fairies had promised.

On the day of her sixteenth birthday, the princess was wandering through the castle when she came to a small room in a tall tower. Inside, an old woman sat spinning thread.

"My dear," cackled the old woman, "come here and try this for yourself."

As soon as the princess's hand touched the spindle, she pricked her finger and fell down on the floor in a deep sleep.

When they discovered their daughter, the king and queen were heartbroken, for they knew that she would not wake for a hundred years. They called for the palace guards, who gently laid the sleeping princess on a golden stretcher and carried her to the royal bedchamber. There they placed her on a bed with silken pillows and velvet covers. The king and queen watched over her and cried.

"Oh, my dear," said the queen to her husband. "How are we ever going to cope without our darling daughter?"

The fairy who had saved the princess's life heard what had happened. Worried that the princess would wake up in a world where she knew no one, she cast a spell over the whole castle. Everyone, from the guards and the kitchen maids to the gardeners and the cooks – even the princess's pet dog – fell into a deep, deep sleep.

Then the fairy made tall trees and sharp brambles grow around the castle, surrounding it with a thick thorny wall that no one could get through. Only the very tops of the castle's towers could be seen.

And so a hundred years went by.

One day, a prince from a nearby land was out riding when he saw the tops of the castle towers rising from the middle of the thick, dark wood. He asked some of the country people about it, and they told him the story of the Sleeping Beauty.

"Many people have wanted to get through those thorns," they told him, "but they have all died trying."

The prince was determined to be the one who succeeded and set off towards the mysterious castle. To the prince's amazement, the thorny brambles and the twisting branches of the dark trees let him

pass through easily. He reached the castle door, and went inside.

The prince walked through many halls and chambers where people and animals slept as if they were dead. He searched every room and chamber, until he found the very one where the beautiful princess slept.

"Oh, princess!" cried the prince. "You are more beautiful than the most delicate rose ever found."

The prince moved quietly towards the sleeping princess and gazed down lovingly at her. He gently took her tiny hand in his, and as love filled his heart, he knelt beside her and slowly kissed her red lips. Instantly the princess's eyes opened.

"Is it you, my prince?" she asked. "I have waited such a long time for you!"

At that moment the spell was broken, and everyone else in the castle woke up, too.

That evening, the princess's sixteenth birthday was celebrated with a joyous party – just a hundred years too late!

The princess and her prince danced together all evening, and, soon after, they were married. They lived together in happiness for many, many years.

# Rise and Shine Bear

"Wakey wakey, rise and shine!" said Mummy Bear. "It's time for school! But if you hurry," said Mummy Bear, "you can play your drums while you get ready."

"Hurray!" cried Teddy Bear, suddenly wide awake. He leaped out of bed and strapped on his shiny blue drum kit.

"One beat for getting up!" he said. "And two beats for getting washed. Three beats for getting dressed. Four beats for marching down to breakfast. And five beats because we're having pancakes – yummy!"

"Now stop drumming and eat your breakfast," said Mummy Bear.

Teddy Bear put his drum on the table, but every now and then he gave it a soft tap with his fingers.

"It's getting late," said Mummy Bear, looking at the clock. "Why don't you wake up Daddy Bear?"

"Wakey wakey, rise and shine!" shouted Teddy Bear happily and loudly — poor Daddy Bear!

# Hungry Bear

"I'm hungry!" said Teddy Bear.

"You've just finished your lunch," said Mummy Bear. "You can have something in a little while."

"But I want something now!" wailed Teddy Bear. "I'm starving!"

"If you eat any more you'll go pop!" said Mummy Bear.

"I only want a biscuit! Or ice cream. Or maybe a piece of cake. I'm really hungry!" grumbled Teddy Bear. He went outside and made hungry faces through the window.

"You don't look hungry," said Betty Bear from next door.

"I am!" said Teddy Bear. Nobody else came by, so Teddy Bear climbed into his sandpit. He dug some roads and built a few houses. He built a huge castle on a hill, with a moat around it. Then he fetched some water from the garden tap and filled the moat.

"Teddy!" called Mummy Bear. "You can come inside now and have some cakes!" But Teddy Bear just shook his head – he was having far too much fun to feel hungry any more!

# The Ugly Duckling

Once upon a time, there was a mother duck who laid a clutch of six beautiful little eggs. One day, she looked into her nest in amazement. There were her six small eggs, but there was another egg that was much bigger than the others. "That's odd," she thought as she sat on the nest.

Soon, one by one, the smaller eggs hatched, and out came six pretty yellow ducklings. Yet the bigger egg still had not hatched.

The mother duck sat on the large egg for another day and another night until at last the egg cracked, and the seventh duckling appeared.

But this one was very different. He was big, with scruffy grey feathers and large brown feet.

"You do look different from my other chicks," exclaimed the mother duck, "but never mind. I'm sure you've got a heart of gold." And she cuddled him to her with all the other ducklings.

Sure enough, he was very sweet-natured and happily played alongside the other ducklings.

One day, the mother duck led her ducklings down to the river to learn to swim. One by one they jumped into the water and splashed about. But when the big grey duckling leaped into the water he swam beautifully. He could swim much faster and further than any of his brothers or sisters. All the other ducklings became very jealous and began to resent him.

"You're a big ugly duckling," they hissed at him. "You don't belong here." And when their mother wasn't looking they chased him right away.

The ugly duckling felt very sad as he waddled away across the fields. "I know I'm not fluffy and golden like my brothers and sisters," he said to himself. "I may have scruffy grey feathers and big brown feet, but I'm just as good as they are – and I'm better at swimming!" He sat down under a bush and started to cry. Just then he heard a sound. Only a short way from where he was hiding, a dog rushed past him, sniffing the ground. The ugly duckling did not dare to move. He stayed under the bush until it was dark and only then did he feel it was safe to come out.

He set off, not knowing which way to go until, along the road, he saw a cosy-looking cottage with lights shining in the windows.

The ugly duckling looked inside cautiously. He could see a fire burning in the hearth and sitting by the fire was an old woman with a hen and a cat.

"Come in, little duckling," said the old woman. "You are welcome to stay here."

The ugly duckling was glad to snuggle down to warm himself by the fire. When the old lady had gone to bed, the hen and the cat cornered the duckling.

"Can you lay eggs?" enquired the hen.

"No," replied the duckling.

"Can you catch mice?" demanded the cat.

"No," replied the miserable duckling.

"Well, you're no use then, are you?" they sneered.

The next day, the old woman scolded the duckling: "You've been here a whole day and not one egg! You're no use, are you?"

So the ugly duckling waddled off out of the cottage. "I know when I'm not wanted," he said to himself mournfully.

He wandered along for a very long time until at last he reached a lake where he could live without anyone to bother him. He lived there for many months. Gradually the days got shorter and the nights longer. The wind blew the leaves off the trees. Winter came and the weather turned bitterly cold. The lake froze over and the ugly duckling shivered under the reeds at the lake's edge. He was desperately cold, hungry and lonely, but he had nowhere else to go.

At last spring came, the weather got warmer and the ice on the lake melted. The ugly duckling felt the sun on his feathers. "I think I'll go for a swim," he thought. He swam right out into the middle of the lake, where the water was as clear as a mirror. He looked down at his reflection in the

water and stared and stared. Staring back at him was a beautiful white bird with a long, elegant neck. "I'm no longer an ugly duckling," he said to himself, "but what am I?"

At that moment three big white birds just like himself flew towards him and landed on the lake. They swam right up to him and one of them said, "You are the handsomest swan that we have ever seen. Would you care to join us?"

"So that's what I am – I'm a swan," thought the bird that had been an ugly duckling. "I would love to join you," he said to the other swans. "Am I really a swan?" he asked, not quite believing it could be true.

"Of course you are!" replied the others. "You're just like us!"

The three older swans became his best friends and the ugly duckling, that was now a beautiful swan, swam across the lake with them and there they lived together. He knew that he was one of them and that he would never be lonely again.

# Hazel Squirrel
## Learns a
## Lesson

Hazel Squirrel had the finest tail of all the animals that lived beside Looking-Glass Pond.

It was fluffier than Dilly Duck's tail… bushier than Harvey Rabbit's tail… and swooshier than everybody's!

Each morning Hazel groomed her tail and admired her reflection in the pond. "I really do have a beautiful tail!" she would say, smiling at herself in the silvery water.

Sometimes Hazel played with her friends, but it usually ended in tears.

"You splashed my lovely tail!" Hazel would shout crossly, when she played leap-frog with Webster. "You're getting my tail dirty, Harvey!"

she would moan very grumpily, when they played digging.

Soon, Hazel stopped playing with her friends altogether. "I'm far too busy brushing my tail!" she said when they came to call. "Come back some other time."

One morning as usual, Hazel was admiring her tail by the pond. Suddenly, she had a funny thought. She couldn't remember the last time she had seen her friends.

Hazel looked at her reflection in the pond. Staring back was a strange face... a cross face... a grumpy face. It was Hazel's face! Hazel couldn't believe her eyes. "No wonder my friends don't visit me," she cried. "I've forgotten how to smile!"

The next day Hazel called for her friends. They had such fun playing leap-frog and digging muddy holes that she forgot all about her tail. "From now on," she laughed, "the only time I'll look at my reflection is to practise smiling!"

# The Boy Who Wished too Much

There once was a young boy named Billy. He was a lucky lad, for he had parents who loved him, plenty of friends and a room full of toys. Behind his house was a rubbish tip. Billy had been forbidden to go there by his mother, but he used to stare at it out of the window. It looked such an exciting place to explore.

One day, Billy was staring at the rubbish tip, when he saw something gold-coloured gleaming in the sunlight. There, on the top of the tip, sat a brass lamp. Now Billy knew the tale of Aladdin, and he wondered if this lamp could possibly be magic, too. When his mother wasn't looking he slipped out of the back door, scrambled up the tip and snatched the lamp from the top.

Billy ran to the garden shed. It was quite dark inside, but Billy could see the brass of the lamp glowing softly in his hands. When his eyes had grown accustomed to the dark, he saw that the lamp was quite dirty. As he started to rub at the brass, there was a puff of smoke and the shed was filled with light. Billy closed his eyes tightly and, when he opened them again, he found to his astonishment that there was a man standing there, dressed in a costume richly embroidered with gold and jewels. "I am the genie of the lamp," he said. "Are you by any chance called Aladdin?"

"N... n... no, I'm Billy," stammered Billy, staring in disbelief.

"How very confusing," said the genie frowning. "I was told that the boy with the lamp was named Aladdin. Oh well! Now I'm here, I may as well grant you your wishes. You can have three, by the way."

At first Billy was so astonished he couldn't speak. Then he began to think hard. What would be the very best thing to wish for? He had an idea. "My first wish," he said, "is that I can have as many wishes as I want."

The genie looked rather taken aback, but then he smiled and said, "A wish is a wish. So be it!"

Billy could hardly believe his ears. Was he really going to get all his wishes granted? He decided to start with a really big wish, just in case the genie changed his mind later. "I wish I could have a purse that never runs out of money," he said.

Hey presto! There in his hand was a purse with five coins in it. Without remembering to thank the genie, Billy ran out of the shed and down the road to the sweet shop. He bought a large bag of sweets and took one of the coins out of his purse to pay for it. Then he peeped cautiously inside the purse, and sure enough there were still five coins. The magic had worked! Billy ran back to the garden shed to get his next wish, but the genie had vanished. "That's not fair!" cried Billy, stamping his foot. Then he remembered the lamp. He seized it and rubbed at it furiously. Sure enough, the genie reappeared.

"Don't forget to share those sweets with your friends," he said. "What is your wish, Billy?"

This time Billy, who was very fond of sweet things, said, "I wish I had a house made of chocolate!"

No sooner had he uttered the words than he found that he was standing outside a house made of rich, creamy chocolate. Billy nibbled at the door knocker. Yes, it was made of delicious chocolate! Billy gorged himself until he felt sick. He lay down on the grass and closed his eyes. When he opened them again, the chocolate house had vanished and he was outside the garden shed once more. "It's not fair to take my chocolate house away. I want it back!" he complained, stamping his foot once again.

Billy went back into the shed. "This time I'll ask for something that lasts longer," he thought. He rubbed the lamp and there stood the genie again.

This time Billy wished for a magic carpet to take him to faraway lands. No sooner were the words out of his mouth than he could feel himself being lifted up and out of the shed on a lovely soft carpet. The carpet took Billy up, up and away over hills, mountains and seas to the ends of the Earth. He saw camels in the desert and polar bears at the North Pole. But eventually, Billy began to feel homesick and he asked the magic carpet to take him home.

Billy was beginning to feel very powerful and important. He began to wish for more and more things. He wished that he did not have to go to school – and so he didn't! He wished for a servant and a cook, and they appeared! Billy began to get very fat and lazy. His parents despaired at how spoiled he had become. His friends no longer came to play because he had grown so boastful.

One morning, Billy woke up and burst into tears. "I'm so lonely and unhappy!" he wailed. He realised that there was only one thing to do. He ran down to the garden shed, picked up the lamp and rubbed it.

"You don't look very happy," said the genie, giving him a concerned glance. "What is your wish?"

"I wish everything was back to normal," Billy blurted out, "and I wish I could have no more wishes!"

"A wise choice!" said the genie. "So be it. Your wish is my command! Goodbye, Billy!" And with that the genie vanished. Billy stepped out of the shed, and from then on everything was normal again. His parents cared for him, he went to school and his friends came to play once more. But Billy had learned his lesson. He never boasted again and he always shared his sweets and all his toys with his friends.

# All at Sea

It was a lovely spring day when Dippy Duckling peeked out of her warm nest at the shimmering river. How cool and inviting the water looked. Soon she was swimming along happily, calling out to all the animals that lived on the riverbank as she went by. She didn't realise how fast or how far the current was carrying her as she swept along past forests and fields.

As Dippy floated on enjoying the warm sun on her back Sally Seagull flew by, squawking loudly. "I've never seen a bird like that on the river before," thought Dippy, in surprise. Then, just as she came round a great bend in the river, she saw the wide, shining ocean spread out in front of her! Dippy began to shake with terror – she was going to be swept out to sea! She started to paddle furiously against the tide, but it was no use. The current was too strong. Just then, a friendly face popped up nearby. It was Ollie Otter. He was very surprised to find Dippy so far from home.

"Climb on my back," he said. Soon his strong legs were pulling them back up the river and safely home.

"Thank you, Ollie," said Dippy. "Without you, I'd be all at sea!"

# Beauty and the Beast

Once upon a time there was a man who lived in a cottage hidden deep in the countryside with his three daughters. His youngest daughter was so pretty that everyone called her "Beauty", which made her two sisters very angry and jealous.

One day the man had to go to the city. Before he left, he told his daughters that he would bring each of them back a present and asked what they would like.

"Jewels!" the eldest daughter demanded. "Silk dresses!" said the second daughter. But all Beauty asked for was a single white rose.

On his return home, the father was caught in a snowstorm and lost his way. The blizzard was so thick and fierce and the forest so large and dark that he nearly gave up hope of ever finding his home. Then, through the swirling mist, he glimpsed a grand palace.

He staggered to the great door – there seemed to be no one about. Inside, he found a table laid with a magnificent dinner. The man ate hungrily, then searched the house. Upstairs, he found a huge bed where he gratefully fell into an exhausted sleep. In the morning, when he awoke, breakfast was waiting beside the bed.

As he set off on his way home he noticed a wonderful rose garden. Remembering Beauty's request, he stopped to pick a single white rose.

Suddenly, with a mighty roar, a terrifying, snarling Beast appeared.

"I have welcomed you with every comfort," he growled, "and in return you steal my roses!"

Shaking with fear, the man begged for forgiveness. "I only wanted the rose as a present for my daughter!"

"I will spare you," said the Beast, "but only if your daughter comes to live here of her own free will. If not, you must return in three months."

Back home, the man tearfully told his daughters what had happened. To his surprise, Beauty agreed to go.

When she arrived at the palace, a glorious meal was waiting for her. "The Beast must want to fatten me," she thought. But she sat and ate.

As soon as Beauty finished her meal, the Beast appeared. He was truly horrifying, and she was frightened.

"Your room is all ready," said the Beast, and he led her to a door that said "Beauty's Room" in gold letters.

The room was everything Beauty could have wished for. She saw a little piano, beautiful silk dresses and fresh, fragrant roses. On the dressing table was a mirror with these words on it:

*If anything you long to see,*
*Speak your wish, and look in me.*

"I wish I could see my father," said Beauty, and instantly saw her father in the mirror, sitting sadly beside the fire at home.

"Perhaps the Beast doesn't mean to kill me after all," Beauty thought. "I wonder what he does want?"

The next evening the Beast joined Beauty for supper. "Tell me," he said, "am I truly horrible to look at?"

Beauty could not lie. "You are," she said. "But I know you are very kind-hearted."

"Then," said the Beast, "will you marry me?"

Beauty was surprised. She knew he might be angry if she refused, but she couldn't say yes because she didn't love him. "No," she said, "I will not marry you."

The Beast sighed so heavily that the walls shook. "Good night, then," he said sadly. And he left her to finish her dinner alone.

Months passed, and the Beast gave Beauty everything she could want. She was very happy in the palace.

Every evening, the Beast asked the same question: "Will you marry me?" And Beauty always said no. But she was growing very fond of him.

One day, Beauty looked in the magic mirror and saw that her father was ill. She begged the Beast to let her go home, and sadly he agreed.

"Take this magic ring," he told her. "If you ever want to come back, put it by your bedside, and when you wake up, you will be here."

"I will come back," Beauty promised.

So Beauty went home to look after her father. He was soon well again, and she was ready to go back to the Beast. But her jealous sisters hated to think of Beauty going back to a palace while they lived in a small cottage. So they convinced her to stay a while longer.

One night, Beauty dreamt that the Beast was lying dead in his garden, and she woke up in tears. She knew then that she loved the Beast, and had to return to him.

Putting the magic ring by her bedside, Beauty lay down again and closed her eyes.

When she opened them again, Beauty was back in the Beast's garden – and, true to her dream, he was lying lifeless on the ground.

"Oh, Beast," she cried, taking him in her arms, "please don't die! I love you, and I want to marry you!"

All at once light and music filled the air, and the Beast vanished. In his place stood a handsome prince.

"Who are you?" cried Beauty.

"I was your Beast," said the prince. "An evil witch cast a spell on me and turned me into that poor animal. The spell could only be broken when a beautiful girl agreed to marry me."

A few days later they were married, and Beauty's family came to join in the joyous celebrations at the palace.

Beauty had never been so happy. She loved the prince with all her heart, and they lived in their rose palace happily ever after.

# The Princess of Hearts

Princess Ruby was given her name because she was born with ruby red lips the shape of a tiny heart. She became a beautiful young lady, with coal black hair, green eyes and skin as pale as milk. She was charming and friendly, but she insisted that everything she owned was heart-shaped! Her bed was heart-shaped, her table and chair were heart-shaped, her maid even brought her sandwiches at teatime cut into the shape of hearts!

As soon as she was old enough, the king and queen wanted Princess Ruby to find a husband. "There is a prince in the next kingdom who is looking for a wife," they told her. "He is brave and handsome and rich. Everything a princess could wish for."

But the foolish princess declared: "I will only marry this prince if he can change the stars in the sky to hearts!"

When Prince Gallant came to visit Princess Ruby she liked his kindly eyes and pleasant smile. They spent the afternoon walking in the palace gardens, and talking about everything under the sun.

But Prince Gallant could not promise to change the stars. As she watched the prince leave, Princess Ruby wished she had not been so foolish!

Prince Gallant, too, was unhappy as he rode home. Suddenly, he heard a screeching sound. In a forest clearing, a dragon was attacking a peacock. The prince took out his sword and chased the dragon away.

The prince was astonished when the peacock spoke. "Thank you for saving me," he said. "I have magical powers," explained the peacock. "But the dragon pulled out my magic feathers, and now I am very weak!"

The Prince gathered up the peacock's feathers. When the feathers had been returned, the peacock gave a loud cry and spread his huge tail wide. "Before I go, I will grant you a single wish," he told the prince. Prince Gallant wished that the stars in the sky would take on the shape of hearts!

Later that night Princess Ruby looked out of the window at the full moon and fields beyond the palace. Then she glanced at the stars – and couldn't believe her eyes! Every single one was in the shape of a heart!

At that moment Prince Gallant appeared on his horse. The prince again asked Princess Ruby if she would marry him – of course she happily agreed! They were married on a lovely summer's day. And, when Princess Ruby made her wedding vows, she promised never to ask for anything foolish, ever again!

# At the Monster Café

Down at the Monster Café there are sights you just would not believe! Monsters love their food, their portions are huge and the colours are scary. As for the ingredients, it might be better not to know, as you will see!

A monster stew is a grisly mixture of turnip tops and vile black drops! They eat rats' tails, slugs and snails, with lots of little flies for decoration.

As for the favourite monster drink – it is lime green, mauve and pink, and made with peas and dead gnat's knees. They say that this goes particularly well with the favourite monster sweets. These are made of dragons' feet, with sugared claws and chocolate paws – gruesome isn't it?

Monster snacks start to bubble when you take off the wrapper. They are made from tar and bits of car, which sounds more like torture than a treat! Fortunately most monsters have very large, sharp teeth so they can munch away merrily on their snacks without breaking them.

The most frightening part of the monster menu is the price list – it is very expensive to eat at the Monster Café. But to a monster it is a real treat. Will you be saving up for a visit?

# Cooking Up a Storm

Wizards love to cook. They have a cauldron for mixing their magic potions, which means they also have all they need to create huge and wonderful stews for their wizard friends.

There is a difference between what you or I might think of as a stew, and what a stew might be to a wizard. We can go to a local shop to buy our ingredients whereas a wizard goes to a pond! The favourite wizard stew is called Storm and, when you know what goes in it, you will see why!

First the wizard has to put a handful of cat's whiskers into a cauldron of boiling dirty pond water. Then he adds the tails from three young pups, a big ladle of eyeballs and two cups of froggy slime. This is stirred slowly for seventeen minutes before adding giant fireworks, a bunch of old tin cans, a pair of cymbals and a big bass drum. Then the windows start to shake and the sky darkens – here comes the storm that goes with the stew! As it rains cats and dogs, and a shower of nasty frogs, the stew is ready… the wizard has cooked up a storm!

# The Bunny Olympics

Everyone on Fiddlestick Farm was really excited – today was the Bunny Olympics. Rabbits hopped and skipped from all around, to find out who would be the champion runner, jumper and muncher!

All the animals helped to put out the plant pots for the Hopping-In-and-Out Race. Then, it was time to start... READY, STEADY, GO!

BOING! BOING! Up and down, in and out of the plant pots they went, as fast as they could! Charlie won, but he had to go back because his little sister Bubbles, was stuck in the first pot!

Next, it was time for the High Jump. Cow and Horse held the rope, while the bouncy bunnies jumped higher and higher until... WHEEEE! Ellie Bunny leapt right over Horse's back!

"No one can jump higher than that!" mooed Cow. "Ellie wins the High Jump!"

In the meadow, near the stream, rabbits were competing in the Long Jump competition. Suddenly – SPLOOSH! Freddie Bunny leapt so far, he landed straight in the water! No one else could jump that far, so he was the winner!

The Munching Contest was next. Sheep was in charge of counting how many carrots and lettuces had been eaten. Patty Bunny munched eight carrots. Little Bobo ate three lettuces and Nicky Bunny chomped through ten carrots and five lettuces. Then – "BUUUURP!" burped Harry, the biggest bunny, very loudly. "Pardon me," he said.

"Goodness!" said Sheep. "Why, Harry, you've gobbled twenty carrots and ten whole lettuces! You are our Champion Muncher!"

Finally, it was time for the Obstacle Race. All the rabbits lined up at the start. The farm animals cheered as the bunnies hopped, bounced and skipped over the stream. They squeezed under the strawberry nets, hopped over the bales of hay and, huffing and puffing, dashed back to the old tractor and past the finishing line. But who was the winner?

They all were! Every one of the bunnies had crossed the finish line together, so they all shared the first prize – a great, big, juicy carrot! And, as the sun began to set, everyone agreed it had been a great Bunny Olympics!

# The Fox and the Grapes

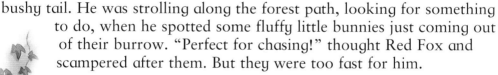

One warm summer's day, Red Fox went out into the forest. He was a handsome young fox and very proud of his thick red coat and fine bushy tail. He was strolling along the forest path, looking for something to do, when he spotted some fluffy little bunnies just coming out of their burrow. "Perfect for chasing!" thought Red Fox and scampered after them. But they were too fast for him.

"You can't catch us!" they giggled, as they darted away.

"Who cares about a bunch of silly bunnies?" thought Red Fox. "Rabbits are never any fun. I'll look for something else to chase!"

So, Red Fox plodded slowly along the path, until he spotted two bushy-tailed squirrels, busily burying acorns. But the squirrels heard Red Fox and scampered quickly away before he could get near them!

"You can't catch us!" they chuckled, as they pelted him with acorns.

"Oh, who cares about a couple of very silly squirrels?" thought Red Fox. "If I had caught them, they would have given me nothing but trouble. I'll find something else to do!"

So, Red Fox continued until he came to the edge of the forest. "I've never been out in the big, wide world," he thought. "I'll bet I can have lots of fun out there!" Red Fox strolled across a field until he came to a wide, dusty road. "I wonder where this leads," he thought, so he decided to follow it.

As he walked, Red Fox looked all around him. He saw some fuzzy field mice, scurrying through the tall grass and then suddenly he heard a loud rumbling and clattering that made the ground shake and made his toes tingle. Red Fox was frightened! He had never heard such a terrible noise before and he wondered if the earth was going to swallow him up!

He crouched down and covered his ears with his paws, but it was only a farmer's cart. As soon as it passed, everything was quiet again and Red Fox went on his way. As Red Fox trudged along, the blazing sun beat down on his back.

He soon grew hot and thirsty and, before long, his empty tummy began to rumble and grumble. "I haven't eaten anything for hours," moaned Red Fox. "And the hot sun and dusty road have made my mouth so dry, I wish I could find something sweet and juicy to eat." Suddenly, Red Fox smelled something wonderful. It was sweet and tempting and it made his mouth water.

He followed his nose across the road, right to where the smell was coming from. Red Fox found himself in the garden of a tiny house. At the side of the house was a leafy grape vine, with big bunches of ripe, purple grapes hanging down. Red Fox couldn't believe his luck!

"Yum, yum!" said Red Fox, licking his lips. "What a delicious smell! Those grapes look so sweet and juicy. They are just what I need to quench my thirst and fill my empty tummy! I'll have to really stretch myself to reach them," said Red Fox, "but I'm sure I can do it!" He stood under the grape vine and reached up as far as he could.

He stretched and stretched and stretched. But even standing on the very tip-toes of his hind legs, Red Fox couldn't reach the grapes. He stretched and stretched again, and wibbled and wobbled, but still he couldn't reach.

"Stretching won't work," grumbled Red Fox. "I know, I'll just have to jump!" So, he jumped high into the air. But he still couldn't reach the grapes. Once again, Red Fox looked up at the grapes, which hung just out of his reach. They looked more delicious than ever and Red Fox knew he had to have some, no matter what it took.

"I must jump higher this time," he thought. So, he concentrated really hard and then leapt up into the air, just as high as he could. But he still couldn't reach those plump, juicy grapes! Red Fox was tired with thirst and hunger, but he couldn't give up now. All his efforts had made him even thirstier, and the grapes looked sweeter and juicier than ever.

"I'll try to reach them one more time," he said. "And this time, I'm sure I will reach them! Then, at last, I will be able to fill my tummy and quench my thirst!" Red Fox reared back on his hind legs and sprang high into the air. But he crashed back to the ground, empty handed. He could not reach those gorgeous grapes.

Exhausted and miserable, Red Fox finally gave up. With his head hanging down, he slowly slunk off down the hot, dusty road.

"Oh, who wants a bunch of silly grapes?" he said. "They were probably sour, anyway!"

And, hungrier and thirstier than ever, he trudged wearily back to the forest.

# Cuddles
## to the
# Rescue

Cuddles was a very smart little poodle. Her hair was snowy white and fell in perfect curls. Her claws were always neatly trimmed and polished. She wore a crisp red bow on top of her head. Once a week Cuddles was sent to the poodle parlour, where she was given a wash, cut and blow dry. And every morning Gilly, her owner, brushed and styled her hair until she looked exactly like herself. But although Cuddles was the smartest, most pampered pooch around, she was not happy. You see, she didn't have any doggy friends. Cuddles tried her best to make friends but the other dogs didn't want to know her.

"Here comes Miss Snooty," they would bark. Then they'd point and snigger, before racing away for some playful puppy fun.

Cuddles would have loved to run around with the other dogs. She thought that chasing sticks and balls looked like brilliant fun. And she was sure that she'd be able to swim in the lake if only she could try. The other dogs didn't know that Cuddles wanted to be one of them, they looked at her and just thought that she was too posh for them.

"She doesn't want to get her paws dirty,"
Mrs Collie explained to Skip, her youngest pup,
when he asked why Cuddles was always on a lead.

Then one day, Cuddles was walking with Gilly
in the park, when she saw Skip chasing ducks
beside the lake. Then, as a duck took off, Skip took
an extra large bounce, and threw himself into the lake.

"Stop!" barked Cuddles. But it was no good, Skip was already up to
his chin in water.

"Help, help!" barked Skip, as he splashed about in the lake. Cuddles,
using all her strength, pulled the lead from Gilly's hand. Gilly looked on
in horror as Cuddles caught the struggling pup by the scruff of his neck
and pulled him ashore. Then, Cuddles gave herself a big shake, then
started to lick Skip dry.

"Cuddles!" cried Gilly, pointing in horror at her soaking wet curls and
muddy paws.

"Will you play with me?" barked
Skip, wagging his tail hopefully.

After that, Gilly always let
Cuddles play with the other dogs
in the park, and Cuddles was the
happiest little poodle around.

# Puss in
# Boots

There was once a miller who had three sons. When he died, he left his mill to the eldest son, his cottage to his middle son and only his pet cat to his youngest son, William.

William went and sat under a tree, feeling very miserable and sorry for himself. "What will become of us, Puss?" he moaned.

To William's utter amazement, Puss answered him. "Don't worry, Master," said the cat. "Just do what I say and you will be far richer than either of your brothers!" Puss told William to get him a fine suit of clothes, a pair of soft leather boots and a strong canvas sack. Then he caught a huge rabbit, put it in the sack, and took it to the palace.

No one at the palace had seen a talking cat, so he was immediately granted an audience with the king.

"Your Majesty," said Puss, "this fine rabbit is a gift from my master, the Marquis of Carabas."

The king had never heard of the Marquis of Carabas, but he was too embarrassed to admit this. "Please thank the Marquis," he said to Puss, "and give him my regards."

The next day, Puss caught some plump partridges and once more he took them to the king, with the same message: "These are from my master."

For several months, Puss went on bringing the king fine gifts.

One day, he heard that the king would be riding along the river bank that afternoon with the princess.

"Master," said Puss, "you must go swimming in the river today."

"Why?" asked William.

"Just do as I say, and you will see," answered Puss.

While William was swimming, Puss hid all his clothes. Then, when he saw the king's carriage approaching, he ran up to it shouting for help. "Help!" cried Puss. "Robbers have stolen my master's clothes!"

When the king recognised the cat, he immediately called to his chief steward and ordered him to bring a fine new suit from the palace.

"It must be of the very finest cut," said the king, "and made from the softest cloth, do you hear! Only the very best will do for the Marquis of Carabas!"

William looked handsome when he was dressed in his fine new suit. The princess invited him to join her and her father in the carriage.

As William and the princess sat next to each other, they began to fall in love.

Meanwhile, Puss ran ahead until he came to a meadow where he saw some men mowing. "The king's carriage is coming," Puss told them. "When he asks whose meadow this is, say it belongs to the Marquis of Carabas – or you will have your heads cut off!"

The mowers didn't dare to disobey. When the royal carriage came by, the king asked who the meadow belonged to. The mowers quickly replied, "The Marquis of Carabas."

"I can see that you are very well-off indeed," the king said to William, who blushed modestly. That made the princess love him even more!

Further on, Puss came to a field where men were harvesting corn.

"When the king asks whose corn this is," Puss told them, "say it belongs to the Marquis of Carabas – or you will have your heads cut off!"

The harvesters didn't dare to disobey.

Next, Puss came to an enormous castle which he knew belonged to a fierce ogre. Still he bravely knocked on the door.

When the ogre let him in, Puss bowed low and said, "I have heard that you have wondrous powers, and can change yourself into anything – even a lion or an elephant."

"That is true," said the ogre. And to prove it, he changed himself into a snarling, growling lion.

Puss was terrified and leapt up onto a cupboard. Then the ogre changed himself back again.

"That was amazing," Puss remarked. "But I am sure it cannot be too difficult for someone of your size to change into a creature as big as a lion.

If you were truly the magician they say you are, you could turn into something tiny – like a mouse."

"Of course I can do that!" bellowed the ogre. In an instant he became a little brown mouse scurrying across the floor.

Quick as a flash, Puss leapt off the cupboard, pounced on the mouse and ate it in one big gulp!

Soon, Puss heard the king's carriage drawing near and rushed outside. As it approached, he bowed low and said, "Welcome, Your Majesty, to the home of the Marquis of Carabas."

The king was very impressed. "May we come in?" he asked.

"Of course, Your Majesty," replied William, looking a little confused.

As they walked through the castle, the king was delighted to see treasures of great value everywhere he looked. He was so pleased that he said to William, "You are the perfect husband for my daughter."

William and the princess were very happy and later that day they were married. They lived in the ogre's castle happily ever after. Puss, of course, lived with them – though he never chased mice again!

# If You Hold My Hand

"Come on, Oakey," his mum called from the front door. "Let's go and explore." But Oakey wasn't sure, the world looked big and scary.

"Only if you promise to hold my hand," said Oakey.

So Oakey's mum led him down the long lane, holding his hand. "This looks like a great playground, especially this slide. Would you like to try?" asked Oakey's mum.

Oakey saw the ladder stretch right up to the sky.

"I'm only small," said Oakey. "I can't climb that high – unless you hold my hand." And Oakey did it!

"Wheee! Did you see me?" he cried.

"We'll take a short cut through the wood," said Oakey's mum.

"I'm not sure," said Oakey. "It looks dark in there. Well, I suppose we could – will you hold my hand?" And Oakey did it!

"Boo! I scared you!" he cried.

Deep in the wood, Oakey found a stream, shaded by beautiful tall trees.

"Stepping stones, look!" said Oakey's mum. "Could you jump across these?"

"Mmm... maybe," said Oakey. "I just need you to hold my hand, please." And Oakey did it!

One... two... three... four... "Now it's your turn now, Mum," cried Oakey, holding out his hand.

Beyond the wood, Oakey and his mum ran up the hill, and down the other side, all the way down to the sea. "Come on, Oakey," called his mum. "Would you like to paddle in the sea with me?"

But the sea looked very big, and he was only small. Suddenly, Oakey knew that didn't matter at all. He turned to his mum and smiled...

"I can do anything if you hold my hand," he said.

# The Mean King
## and the
# Crafty Lad

There was once a king who was as mean as he was rich. He lived in a great palace where he spent his days counting his bags of gold coins. Meanwhile his subjects lived in great poverty. Sometimes the king would summon his page to prepare the royal carriage. Then the king would set forth in his great, golden coach to survey his kingdom.

Now not only was the king extremely rich, but he was very vain. As he passed his subjects working in the field, he liked them to bow to him and pay him compliments. "How handsome you look today, Your Majesty!" they would call, or "How well the colour pink suits you, Sire!" His head would swell with pride as he moved on. "My people truly adore me!" he would say.

But, for all their complimentary words, the people hated their king. They resented the fact that the king lived in splendour while his subjects toiled hard all their lives. The peasants called a secret meeting. "Let's sign a petition demanding our rights!" cried one man.

"And fair pay!" shouted another. They all cheered and clapped their hands.

"Who's going to write down our demands?" called an old woman. Now the crowd was hushed, for none of them knew how to read or write.

"I know what we can do instead," called a voice from the back. Everyone turned round to see a young lad in rags. "Let's march on the palace!" he cried.

"Yes!" roared the crowd.

As the angry mob reached the palace, the king saw them and sent out his guard dogs. The peasants were forced to flee for their lives with the dogs snapping at their ankles. Not until the last peasant was out of sight did the king call off his dogs.

"Good work!" he cried. From then on, however, life became even harder for the people because the king was on his guard in case they marched on the castle again. Now, when he went out and about in his kingdom, he was always accompanied by his hounds.

Eventually, another secret meeting was called. "What can we do?" the people said. "We will never be able to get past those savage dogs."

"I've got an idea," came a familiar voice. It was the ragged lad again. For a while there was uproar as folk accused him of having nearly lost them their lives. "Please trust me," pleaded the lad. "I know I let you down, but this time I've got a well thought-out plan to get the king to give up his money." In the end, the peasants listened to the boy's scheme and they decided to let him try.

The next day, the boy hid in a branch of a tree that overhung the palace garden. With him he had some dog biscuits, in which he had hidden a powerful sleeping pill. He threw the biscuits on to the palace lawn and waited. Some time later, as the boy had hoped, the king's hounds came out on to the lawn. They headed straight for the biscuits and gobbled them up. Soon they were fast asleep, one and all.

Quickly the lad slid out of the tree and, donning a large black cape, he ran round to the front of the palace and rapped on the door. A sentry opened the door. "Good day," said the lad, "I am Victor, the world-famous vet. Do you have any animals requiring medical attention?"

"No," replied the sentry, slamming the door in the lad's face. Just then voices could be heard from within the palace and the sentry opened the door again saying, "Actually, we do have a problem. Step inside."

The sentry led the lad out to the lawn where the king was weeping over the dogs' bodies. "Oh, please help," he cried. "I need my dogs. Without them I may be besieged by my own people."

The lad pretended to examine the dogs. He said to the king, "I have seen one case like this. The only cure is to feed the animals liquid gold."

"Liquid gold?" exclaimed the king. "Where shall I find it?"

"Fear not," said the lad, "I have a friend – a witch – who lives in the mountains. She can turn gold coins into liquid gold. If you let me take all the dogs to her she will cure them. But you will have to give me a bag of gold to take to her."

Well, the king was so worried that he readily agreed. The sleeping dogs were loaded on to a horse-drawn cart, and the king gave the lad a bag of gold saying, "Hurry back, my dogs are most precious."

The lad went home. His parents helped him unload the dogs, who by now were beginning to wake up. They took great care of the dogs and the next day the lad put on the cloak again and returned to the palace.

"The good news is," he said to the king, "that the cure is working. The bad news is that there was only enough gold to revive one dog. I'll need all the gold you've got to cure the others."

"Take it all," screamed the king, "only I must have my dogs back tomorrow!" He opened the safe and threw his entire stock of gold on to another cart, which the young lad dragged away.

That night the lad gave each of the king's subjects a bag of gold. The next morning he led the dogs back to the palace. To his surprise, the king didn't want them back. "Now I have no gold," he said, "I don't need guard dogs."

Then the lad saw that the king had learned his lesson, and he told the king what had really happened. And, to everyone's joy, the king said the peasants could keep their bags of gold. As for the king, he kept the dogs as pets and became a much nicer person.

# Shanty Goes to Sea

Shanty, the harbour kitten, just loved fish. He ate every scrap that the fishermen threw away. And sometimes, when nobody was looking, he even helped himself to a few whole fish that should have gone to market.

"Don't you ever get tired of fish?" asked his friend Gull. But Shanty just shook his head as he nibbled on a tasty sardine!

One day, Shanty had an idea. "There's only one thing that would be better than being a harbour kitten – being a boat kitten!" he told Gull. "Then I could eat all the fish I wanted."

So the next morning, Shanty crept aboard the *Salty Sardine*, the biggest fishing boat in the harbour. Everybody was so busy that they didn't notice the stowaway hidden beneath an old raincoat. The boat chugged out into a calm sea, and Shanty had a great time dreaming about all the fish that he was going to eat.

When the fishermen started pulling in the nets, Shanty couldn't believe his eyes. There were so many fish that nobody noticed when a few sardines, cod, mackerel and haddock began to disappear under the old raincoat.

Shanty ate and ate, until he could eat no more. Then he curled up for a sleep. But, as he was dozing off, something strange began to happen. The *Salty Sardine* began to creak and moan, and sway and rock. Water sprayed over the sides as it bounced over the waves then crashed back down again. Shanty's head began to reel and his stomach began to roll. Oh, how he wished he hadn't eaten so many fish! Oh, how he wished he'd stayed on dry land!

Soaked right through, Shanty peered out to see what the fishermen were doing. To his surprise, instead of running about and screaming, they were all working. One of them, who Shanty thought must be the captain, was even whistling. And another was eating a sausage roll. It seemed that for them, this was a normal day's work.

When the *Salty Sardine* got back to the harbour, Shanty got off as fast as his wobbly legs would carry him and quickly sat down on dry land.

"How is life as a boat kitten?" asked Gull, when he came visiting later that evening.

"Ah!" said Shanty, after he'd finished nibbling on a scrap of sardine. "Boats are all very well but give me the harbour any day. After all, how many fish can one kitten eat!"

# Clumsy Fred

Clumsy Fred was a very cross giant! Whatever he did became a disaster. He bumped into castles and turned homes into rubble. He sent garden sheds flying and trod on lamp posts as he strode across the town. Everyone ran whenever Clumsy Fred was approaching. They could hear him coming for miles as he crashed and banged his way across the countryside and through the town.

People became more and more concerned. What was the matter with Fred? There was definitely something wrong, but no one was sure how to help. Then a monster expert came to the rescue.

He went to see Fred, who was feeling very sad. "Why am I so clumsy?" he asked. "I don't like upsetting everyone, but I just can't help it!"

The expert did a lot of tests, and found the solution. "I know what is wrong!" he said. "The problem is your eye!"

So Fred put on a monocle and suddenly he could see. He wasn't clumsy any more, and Fred was as happy as can be!

# Oscar Octopus

Oscar Octopus was a keen footballer. With his many feet he was a real menace to the other team. Today was a big match, and he was playing as number eleven.

Oscar began to get ready. He stretched out a tentacle and put on the first boot, then he put on the second. As Oscar put on boot three he heard the crowd singing about Oscar, the latest goal-scoring sensation. As Oscar put on boot four he was feeling on top form. On went boot five as the crowd swayed and cheered loudly. The harder Oscar tried to hurry, the longer it seemed to take! Boot number six went on, and Oscar practised some tricks, then boot seven – he was almost ready. Now it was the last one – boot eight, but the laces were so fiddly that it took him ages.

At last he was ready and on to the pitch he went, ready for his debut in front of the crowd. But the referee said, "Sorry Oscar! You're too late. The game is over, the whistle has blown. Nobody scored and the crowd has gone home!"

# A Perfect Puppy

Polly had wanted a puppy for a long time, so when Mummy and Daddy said yes, she couldn't wait to get to the pet shop.

At the pet shop, Polly inspected the puppies one by one. After all, her puppy had to be perfect.

"That one's too big," said Polly, pointing to a Great Dane. "And that one's too small." She pointed to a tiny Chihuahua. "And that one's too curly," Polly declared, looking at a poodle. Another puppy was too noisy. And one was too quiet.

Before long, there weren't many puppies left. Polly was about to give up, when something soft rubbed against her leg. "Perfect!" she cried, picking up a small bundle of black and white fur.

"Err, what kind of puppy is it?" asked Daddy.

"It's a mongrel," said the shopkeeper. "I think it's part Spaniel and part Collie. We're not really sure."

"I don't care what he is," smiled Polly. "He's just perfect. I'm going to call him Danny."

Danny whined as he left the pet shop. And he whined all the way home. He stopped whining when he saw the cat and barked instead. "He'll be okay once he gets used to us," said Mummy. Polly hoped she was right.

In the afternoon, they all took Danny for a walk. Polly took some bread to feed the ducks, but as soon as Danny saw the ducks he started to bark. Then he began to chase them and didn't stop until they had all flown away.

"He's just a puppy. He's got a lot to learn," explained Daddy. Polly was beginning to wonder if she'd chosen the right puppy.

Later, Polly introduced Danny to her favourite teddy, Mr Fluffy. But he just grabbed him and ran off. When he came back, Mr Fluffy was gone. Polly was furious. She waved an angry finger at Danny. "You're not a perfect puppy," she said. "I don't think you'll ever learn."

Poor Danny, he hung his head and slunk away under the table and wouldn't come out all evening.

The next morning, Polly was woken up by something wet pressed against her cheek. It was Danny, and in his mouth was Mr Fluffy! Danny dropped Mr Fluffy on the floor for Polly to pick up. "Good boy, Danny," laughed Polly, tickling his ears. "You are a perfect puppy, after all!"

# The Golden Bird

There was once a king who kept a golden bird in a gilded cage. The bird wanted for nothing. Every day the king's servant brought him food and water and groomed his fine yellow feathers. And each day the bird sang his beautiful song for the king. "How lucky I am," cried the king, "to have such a beautiful bird that sings such a fine song." However, as time passed the king began to feel sorry for the bird. "It really isn't fair," he thought, "to keep such a handsome creature in a cage. I must give the bird its freedom."

He called his servant and ordered him to take the cage into the jungle and release the bird.

The servant obeyed, and took the cage deep into the jungle where he came to a small clearing. He set the cage down, opened the door and out hopped the golden bird. "I hope you can look after yourself," the servant said as he walked away.

The golden bird looked about him. "This is strange!" he thought to himself. "Still, I suppose someone will come along to feed me soon." He settled down and waited.

After a while he heard a crashing sound in the trees, and then he saw a monkey swinging from branch to branch on his long arms.

"Hello there!" called the monkey, hanging by his tail and casting the bird an upside down grin. "Who are you?"

"I am the golden bird," replied the golden bird haughtily.

"I can see you're new around here," said the monkey. "I'll show you the best places to feed in the tree tops."

"No thanks," replied the golden bird ungratefully. "What could an ape like you possibly teach me? You've got such a funny face. I expect you're envious of my beautiful beak," he added.

"Have it your own way," called the monkey, and swung into the trees.

Some time later the golden bird heard a hissing noise and a snake came slithering by. "Well, hello," hissed the snake. "Who are you?"

"I am the golden bird," replied the golden bird proudly.

"Let me show you the jungle paths," said the snake.

"No thanks," said the bird rudely. "What could a snake possibly teach me? With your horrid hissing voice, you must be jealous of my beautiful song," he said, forgetting that he had not sung yet.

"Very well," hissed the snake as he slithered and slipped his way into the undergrowth.

By now the golden bird was beginning to wonder when his food would arrive. He began to imagine the tasty morsel that he hoped he would soon be eating.

Just then he was aware of a movement on the tree trunk behind him. Looking up he caught a glimpse of a chameleon, lying camouflaged against the trunk.

"Good day," said the chameleon. "I've been here all the time, so I know who you are. You're the golden bird. It's a good idea to know where to hide in case of danger. Let me show you."

"No thanks," replied the golden bird. "What could an ugly brute like you possibly teach me? You must wish you had lovely feathers like me," he said, fluffing up his beautiful, golden plumage.

"Well, don't say I didn't warn you," muttered the chameleon as he darted away.

The golden bird had just settled down again when a great grey shadow passed over the jungle. He looked up to see a great eagle swooping low over the trees. The monkey swung up to hide in the densest foliage near the top of the trees. The snake slid off to hide in the deepest part of the undergrowth. The chameleon stayed quite still but his skin colour became a perfect match for the tree he was on and he became totally invisible.

"Aha!" thought the golden bird. "All I have to do is fly away and that stupid eagle will never catch up with me." He flapped his wings and flapped and flapped, but he did not know that his wings had grown weak through living a life of luxury in the palace. Now the bird regretted his golden plumage and wished that he had dull brown feathers that would not show up in the forest clearing. For his fine yellow feathers made him easy to see. He was sure the eagle would come and gobble him up. "Help!" he trilled. "Please help me someone." Now he could see the eagle swooping down towards him with eyes blazing like fire and talons drawn.

At that moment the golden bird felt something close around his legs and pull him into the undergrowth. It was the snake. Then he was lifted up into the trees by a long, hairy arm and saw he was being carried by the monkey. "Keep still," whispered the chameleon pushing him into the centre of a large yellow flower. "The eagle won't see you there." And sure enough, the golden bird found that he was precisely the colour of the flower and the eagle flew straight past him.

"How can I repay you all?" exclaimed the bird. "You saved my life!"

"You can sing for us," replied the animals. And so from then on, the monkey, the snake and the chameleon looked after the golden bird, and he sang his beautiful song for them every single day.

# Harvey the Shyest Rabbit

Harvey the rabbit was the shyest animal in the glade by Looking-Glass Pond. He was too shy to talk to anyone… too shy to play with the other animals… too shy even to look out from behind his big floppy ears.

"There's no need to be scared," Mama Rabbit told him. "If you want to join in, all you have to do is ask."

But Harvey hid behind the long grass, and no one noticed him at all!

One morning, Harvey was sitting beside Looking-Glass Pond – alone.

"I wish I could make a friend," he sighed. "But how can I, when no one even notices me?"

Then, as he gazed down sadly at the pond, he could hardly believe his eyes! There, in the water was another little rabbit with big floppy ears, staring back at him.

"He looks just as scared as me!" thought Harvey. He smiled shyly at the rabbit in the water, and the water rabbit smiled too! Harvey did a bunny hop in surprise, and the water rabbit did one too. "Hello!" said Harvey bravely.

"Hello!" said the rabbit.

"So that's how you make friends!" cried Harvey, in amazement. "You just need to be a little bit brave."

He was so excited that he raced off to tell everyone his news.

And this time, everyone noticed him! Soon Harvey had lots of new friends to play with. But he never forgot to go back to visit his very first friend in Looking-Glass Pond!

# Goldilocks
## and the
# Three Bears

Once upon a time, deep in a dark green forest, there lived a family of brown bears. There was great big Daddy Bear. There was middle-sized Mummy Bear. And there was little Baby Bear.

One sunny morning, the bears were up early, hungry for their breakfast. Daddy Bear cooked three bowls of porridge. He made it with lots of golden, runny honey, just the way bears like it. "Breakfast is ready!" called Daddy Bear.

But, when he poured it into the bowls, it was far too hot to eat!

"We'll just have to let our porridge cool down for a while before we eat it," said Mummy Bear.

"But I'm hungry!" wailed Baby Bear.

"Let's go for a walk in the forest while we wait," suggested Mummy Bear. "Get the basket, Baby Bear, we can gather some wild berries as we go."

So, leaving the steaming bowls of porridge on the table, the three bears went out into the forest. The last one out was little Baby Bear, and he forgot to close the front door behind him.

The sun was shining brightly that morning and someone else was walking in the forest. It was a little girl called Goldilocks, who had long, curly golden hair and the cutest nose you ever did see.

Goldilocks was skipping happily through the forest when suddenly she smelt something yummy and delicious – whatever could it be?

She followed the smell until she came to the three bears' cottage. It seemed to be coming from inside. The door was open, so she peeped in and saw three bowls of porridge on the table.

Goldilocks just couldn't resist the lovely, sweet smell. So, even though she knew she wasn't ever supposed to go into anyone's house without first being invited, she tiptoed inside.

First, she tasted the porridge in Daddy Bear's great big bowl. "Ouch!" she said. "This porridge is far too hot!" So she tried the porridge in Mummy Bear's middle-sized bowl. "Yuck!" said Goldilocks. "This porridge is far too sweet!" Finally, she tried the porridge in Baby Bear's tiny little bowl. "Yummy!" she said, licking her lips. "This porridge is just right!" So Goldilocks ate it all up – every last drop!

Goldilocks was so full up after eating Baby Bear's porridge that she decided she must sit down. First, she tried sitting in Daddy Bear's great big chair. "Oh, dear!" she said. "This chair is far too hard!" So she tried Mummy Bear's middle-sized chair. "Oh, no!" said Goldilocks. "This chair is far too soft!" Finally, she tried Baby Bear's tiny little chair. "Hurray!" she cried. "This chair is just right!" So she stretched out and made herself very comfortable.

But Baby Bear's chair certainly wasn't just right! It was far too small and, as Goldilocks settled down, it broke into lots of little pieces!

Goldilocks picked herself up off the floor and brushed down her dress. Trying out all of those different chairs had made her very tired. She looked around the cottage for a place to lie down and soon found the three bears' bedroom.

First, Goldilocks tried Daddy Bear's great big bed. "Oh no, this won't do!" she said. "This bed is far too hard!" So she tried Mummy Bear's

middle-sized bed. "Oh, bother!" said Goldilocks. "This bed is far too soft!" Finally, she tried Baby Bear's tiny little bed. "Yippee!" she cried. "This bed is just right!" So Goldilocks climbed in, pulled the blanket up to her chin and fell fast, fast asleep.

Not long after, the three bears came home from their walk, ready for their yummy porridge. But, as soon as they entered their little cottage, they knew something wasn't quite right.

"Someone's been eating my porridge!" said Daddy Bear, when he looked at his great big bowl.

"Someone's been eating my porridge!" said Mummy Bear, looking at her middle-sized bowl.

"Someone's been eating my porridge," cried Baby Bear, looking sadly at his tiny little bowl. "And they've eaten it all up!"

Then Daddy Bear noticed that his chair had been moved. "Look, Mummy Bear! Someone's been sitting in my chair!" he said in his deep, gruff voice.

"Look, Daddy Bear! Someone's been sitting in my chair," said Mummy Bear, as she straightened out the cushions on it.

"Someone's been sitting in my chair, too," cried Baby Bear. "And look! They've broken it all to pieces!" They all stared at the bits of broken chair. Then Baby Bear burst into tears.

Suddenly, the three bears heard the tiniest of noises. Was it a creak? Was it a groan? Where was it coming from? No, it was a snore, and much to their surprise, it was coming from their bedroom. They crept up the stairs very, very slowly and quietly, to see what was making the noise...

"Someone's been sleeping in my bed!" cried Daddy Bear.

"Someone's been sleeping in my bed," said Mummy Bear.

"Someone's been sleeping in my bed!" cried Baby Bear. "And she's still there!"

All this noise woke Goldilocks up with a start.

When she saw the three bears standing over her, Goldilocks was very scared. "Oh, dear! Oh, dear! Oh, dear!" she cried, jumping out of Baby Bear's bed. She ran out of the bedroom, down the stairs, out of the front door and all the way back home – and she never ever came back to the forest again!

# Baby Bear
## Finds a
# Friend

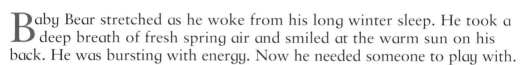

Baby Bear stretched as he woke from his long winter sleep. He took a deep breath of fresh spring air and smiled at the warm sun on his back. He was bursting with energy. Now he needed someone to play with.

Baby Bear bounded over to join some baby bunnies playing, but Mrs Rabbit shooed him off. "Your paws will hurt my babies," she said.

Baby Bear went down to the river, where some beavers were building a dam. But the beavers were too busy to play with Baby Bear.

So he sat watching Kingfisher diving into the water. "That looks like fun!" he said, jumping in with a splash!

"Go away!" said Kingfisher. "You will disturb the fish!"

By now Baby Bear was feeling fed up and tired. He lay down in a hollow and closed his eyes. Then, just as he was drifting to sleep, a voice said, "Will you come and play with me?" He opened his eyes to see another bear cub. Baby Bear smiled.

"I'm too tired to play now," he said. "But I will play with you all day tomorrow!" And from then on, he was never lonely again.

# The Hare and the Tortoise

Hare was the most boastful animal in the whole forest. On this sunny morning, he was trotting down the path singing, "I'm handsome and clever and the fastest hare ever! There's no one as splendid as me!"

Mole, Mouse and Squirrel watched him. "Hare is so annoying," said Mole. "Someone should find a way to stop him boasting all the time!"

"I'll get him to stop!" said Squirrel and he jumped on to the path right in front of Hare. "I'm as handsome as you are, Hare," he said. "Look at my big bushy tail."

"It's not as handsome as my fluffy white tail and my long silky ears!" boasted Hare.

"Well, I'm as clever as you are!" said Mouse, hurrying out to join them. "I can dig holes under trees and store enough nuts and seeds to last all winter!"

"That's nothing!" said Hare. "In winter, I can change my coat to white, so that I can hide in the snow!"

"Now, is there anyone who thinks they can run as fast as me?" said Hare to the animals, who had gathered round. "Who wants a race?" No one said anything! All the animals knew that Hare was very fast and no one thought they could beat him. "Ha!" exclaimed Hare. "That proves it! I'm the handsomest, the cleverest and the fastest."

"Excuse me," said a small voice.

"Yes?" said Hare, turning around.

"I will race you," said Tortoise.

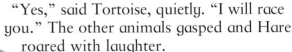

"YOU?" said Hare, in amazement. "The slowest, clumsiest animal on four legs?"

"Yes," said Tortoise, quietly. "I will race you." The other animals gasped and Hare roared with laughter.

"Will you race me to the willow tree?" Hare asked Tortoise.

"Yes," said Tortoise.

"Will you race past the willow tree, to the stream?" asked Hare.

"Yes, I will," said Tortoise.

"Will you race past the willow tree, past the stream and then all the way to the old oak tree?" asked Hare.

"Of course I will," said Tortoise.

"Fine," said Hare. "We'll start at nine o'clock in the morning! I will meet you here, at the big oak tree."

"All right," said Tortoise, and all the other animals ran off to tell their friends the news.

The next morning, everyone had turned out to watch the big race. Some were at the starting line and others were going to the finish, to see who would get there first.

Magpie called, "Ready, steady, GO!" And Tortoise and Hare were off! Hare shot past Tortoise and, when there was no one to show off for, he slowed down just a bit. He reached the willow tree and looked behind him – Tortoise was not in sight!

"It will take him ages just to catch me," Hare thought. "I don't need to hurry. I may as well stop and rest." He sat down under the willow tree and closed his eyes. In minutes, he was fast asleep.

Meanwhile, Tortoise just plodded on. He didn't try to go faster than he could, but he didn't stop, either. He just kept going, on and on and on. The sun climbed higher in the sky and Tortoise felt hot. But he still kept going. His stubby legs were beginning to ache, but he knew he mustn't stop.

Hare kept snoring under the willow tree.

Some time later, Tortoise reached Hare. At first, Tortoise thought that he should wake Hare up. Then he changed his mind.

"Hare is very clever," he told himself. "He must have a reason for sleeping, and I am sure he would only be cross if I woke him!" So, Tortoise left Hare sleeping and went on his way, walking slowly towards the finish line.

Tortoise walked on and on. The finishing line seemed so far away, but the sun was getting lower now and it wasn't as hot. As he plodded along, bees flew along beside tortoise to encourage him on his way.

Later that afternoon the air grew chilly, as the sun faded. The change in the temperature woke Hare with a start.

"The race!" he thought. "I have to finish the race!"

He looked around to see if Tortoise was nearby. There was no sign of him. "Hah!" said Hare. "He still hasn't caught up with me. No need to hurry, then."

And he trotted towards the clearing, with a big grin on his face. When he neared the finish, Hare could hear cheers and clapping.

"They must be able to see me coming," he thought. But, as he got closer, he saw the real reason for all the noise and his heart sank. There was Tortoise, crossing the line. Tortoise had won! The animals were cheering wildly.

As Hare crept up to the finishing line, the cheers turned to laughter. His ears turned bright red and drooped with embarrassment. He had been so foolish to be so boastful! Hare walked off on his own, too ashamed to say anything to anyone.

Meanwhile everyone gathered round to congratulate Tortoise. No one noticed that hare had slipped away. Tortoise was looking rather shy, but very proud. He had proved that slow but steady always wins the race.

# The Clumsy Fairy

D id you know that all fairies have to go to school to learn how to be fairies? They have to learn how to fly, how to be graceful and how to do magic. Clementine found it difficult! Poor Clementine. She was the worst in the class. She was clumsy and awkward. When they were dancing she was the only fairy who tripped over her own feet. At the end of term all the fairies were given a special task for the holidays. But there was one task that no one wanted. This was to help a little girl who had measles.

"Clementine," said Madam Bouquet, "I want you to paint this rose petal lotion on the little girl's spots every night when she is asleep. If you do this for one week, the spots will disappear."

That night Clementine flew in through the little girl's window. So far so good! The little girl's name was Alice, and Clementine could see her fast asleep in bed. She was holding a fat, round teddy in her arms.

Clementine crept towards the bed. Then a toy clown pinched her bottom! "Ouch!" she yelled.

Alice woke up. "Who's there?" she asked sleepily.

"It's Clementine," said the fairy, and explained to Alice why she had come. "I'm sorry I woke you," she added. "You're not really supposed to see me."

Alice didn't mind. It was lovely to talk to a fairy. "Can you really do magic?" she asked Clementine.

"Yes," Clementine told her. "I'm quite good at magic. I just wish I wasn't so clumsy." She told Alice about her dance classes and Alice told Clementine about her ballet lessons.

"If you are helping me get rid of my measles," she said to Clementine, "I'll help you with your ballet." Each night Alice taught Clementine how to point her toes, keep her balance on one foot and curtsy gracefully. But it was the pirouette that Clementine did best of all. Holding her arms high above her head she twirled and twirled round Alice's bedroom.

Each day Clementine painted Alice's spots and by the end of the week they had gone.

After the holidays the fairies went back to school. And, do you know, Clementine was the best dancer in the class. Madam Bouquet couldn't believe her eyes.

"Why, Clementine," she gasped, "you're my prima ballerina!" And "prima", as I'm sure you know, means "first and best"!

Clementine was the happiest fairy in the world!

# You are Not my Best Friend

Gabriella Goat, Chicken Charlotte, Sam the Sheepdog, Penfold Pig, Sally the Sheep and Jersey Cow all lived on Willow Farm. In the late afternoon when all the farm work had been done, they liked to meet in the paddock next to the farmyard to talk.

Gabriella was a very self-important goat, because she thought she was more useful on the farm than all the other animals. Not only did she provide milk for the farmer's wife to make cheese, but she also nibbled all the nettles and weeds and kept the farmyard neat and tidy. As far as she was concerned, that was much more important than just laying eggs or looking after sheep, or helping the farmer look for truffles, growing wool, or making milk.

Each morning, when Chicken Charlotte had finished laying eggs and all the other animals were still hard at work, she would flutter over the picket fence that kept the foxes away and strut over to visit Gabriella.

One very hot day when the sun was shining down on the garden, Gabriella decided she and Chicken Charlotte should go down to the duck pond and soak their feet in the clear, cool water. Chicken Charlotte didn't like this idea at all! "I'm afraid I might fall in and drown," said Chicken Charlotte. "I can't swim."

"You can't swim?" gasped Gabriella Goat. "How can you be any fun if you can't swim?" And she turned her back on Chicken Charlotte. Gabriella thought about who liked swimming, then she smiled. "Sam the Sheepdog can swim," she said. "Sam will be my very best friend."

Sam the Sheepdog had just finished chasing Sally the Sheep into the field when Gabriella Goat called out to him, "How about taking a break now and coming to the duck pond with me?"

"Why not?" Sam asked when he'd got his breath back. "It's a boiling hot day and I could do with a nice long swim to help me cool down."

Gabriella and Sam had tremendous fun all day splashing around in the water, and at the end of the day Gabriella said to Sam, "You're my very best friend. Let's do this again tomorrow!"

Sam agreed. He was delighted that Gabriella liked him the best of all the animals.

The next day, Gabriella went to fetch Sam so that they could play. Sam was in the field chasing Sally but, when Gabriella beckoned for him to come and play, Sam shook his head. "It's too early," said Sam. "I've got to make sure Sally grazes all this field, and the pond is all muddy now. The farmer won't like it if I get too dirty."

"What?" squealed Gabriella Goat in disbelief. "Whoever heard of a dog that didn't like mud?" And with that she turned her back on Sam the Sheepdog. Gabriella thought for a while about who else might like mud, and then smiled triumphantly. "Penfold Pig likes getting muddy," she said. "Penfold Pig will be my very best friend."

Penfold Pig was snuffling around in the hot yard when Gabriella Goat found him. "Come and roll in the mud with me," said Gabriella.

They had such fun that Penfold wanted to do this again the following day, but Gabriella said that she'd had enough of basking now, and tomorrow she wanted to lie in the field and chew juicy grass. Penfold Pig was distraught.

He didn't like chewing grass – he liked pig-swill.
Sadly, he told Gabriella Goat that he'd not be able to join her.

"You'll never make a good best friend if you can't eat grass," huffed Gabriella. And with that she turned her back on Penfold Pig. She thought about who else liked eating grass, and then smiled triumphantly. "Jersey Cow likes eating grass," thought Gabriella Goat. "Jersey Cow will be my very best friend."

The following morning, Gabriella went to find Jersey Cow, who was just about to be milked by the farmer's wife. She told Jersey Cow her plans for the day. Jersey Cow said that she would be honoured to have Gabriella to talk to as they chomped and lazed the day away. "I'll be with you in just a tick," said Jersey Cow. "I need to be milked first."

Gabriella Goat stared at Jersey Cow, and then turned and walked away! "What's wrong with all these silly animals?" she asked herself.

"Why do they have to do something else first, or can't even do something at all?" And with that she decided to go alone to the juicy green field.

When Gabriella got to the field, she spied Sally the Sheep grazing away. Sally the Sheep was very pleased to be chosen as Gabriella's friend, and they spent the next hour talking and munching away. Before very long, Jersey Cow came to join them.

"Friendship is all about giving and taking," remarked Gabriella to Sally the Sheep (so that Jersey Cow could overhear), "and being a very best friend means giving a lot." But, when Jersey Cow moved off to chew some grass a little further away, Sally the Sheep followed her. Gabriella Goat snorted in disgust, and then chewed some more. "Who needs friends anyway?" she thought. "They're no good to anyone."

Gabriella Goat started to feel bored. She wanted to play a game. All the animals were together in the paddock. But, when Gabriella got close, all the animals turned their backs.

Just then she heard Jersey Cow remark to Sally the Sheep, "You know, friendship is all about giving and taking. If a friend of mine wouldn't give as well as take, she'd be no friend of mine."

Gabriella was very upset. She skulked off to the farmyard and was utterly miserable. The more she thought, the more miserable she became. The more miserable she became, the more she realised what a terrible friend she had been. The next day when she saw all her former friends, she sobbed, "I'm so sorry, won't you all forgive me?"

Chicken Charlotte flew to her side and gave her a big hug, and then all the other animals joined in. Nobody had liked seeing her so sad, and they all wanted to be friends again.

"I've been so silly," said Gabriella, "but now I realise that you are ALL my very best friends."

# Where's Wanda?

Sally was worried. Wanda, her cat, was getting fat and she wouldn't sit in her basket. "She must be ill," Sally told her mummy. "Her tummy's all swollen, and she hasn't slept in her basket for days."

"Don't worry," said Mummy, giving Sally a hug. "If she's not better in the morning, we'll take her to the vet."

"Sssh!" whispered Sally. "You know how much Wanda hates the V-E-T." But it was too late, Wanda had already gone, and she didn't appear for her bowl of milk the following morning.

"She must have heard us talking about the vet," said Sally. "Perhaps she's hiding in the garden," she said.

They looked everywhere, but all they found were the birds. "Sometimes she sunbathes in the vegetable patch," said Sally. But the only animal there was a fluffy rabbit.

Wanda was nowhere around the house or garden, so Mummy took Sally to look in the park. "Here, Wanda!" called Sally. But all they found there were dogs. Wanda hated dogs, so she wouldn't be there.

On the way home, Sally even sat on Mummy's shoulders so that she could look on top of people's garages and sheds. "She must have run away!" cried Sally, sadly.

But Mummy had an idea. She helped Sally to draw some pictures of Wanda. Then they wrote MISSING and their telephone number on the pictures. They posted the leaflets through all the letterboxes in the street.

In the afternoon Mrs Jones from next door popped her head over the hedge. "Come and see what I've found in my laundry basket," smiled Mrs Jones. Sally and her mummy rushed next door at once. When Sally saw what Mrs Jones had in her laundry basket she couldn't believe her eyes.

There, sitting amongst the washing, was Wanda. She looked very slim and very proud. And beside her lay five tiny kittens. They were so young that their eyes were still closed. Wanda hadn't been ill after all. She'd been expecting kittens!

Mrs Jones said that they could keep the basket until Wanda had finished with it. So Mummy carried the new family home as Sally skipped beside her. Sally was so excited. She just couldn't wait to tell people how they'd gone searching for one cat and found six!

# The Elves and the Shoemaker

Once upon a time there was a kind old shoemaker who lived in a tiny flat above his shop with his wife. He had many bills to pay, so he had to work from dawn to dusk to pay them off. The day came when he had only a few pennies left – just enough to buy leather for one final pair of shoes.

That evening, by candlelight, the shoemaker cut up the leather. Then, leaving it on his workbench, he picked up his candle and wearily climbed the stairs to his bed.

The next morning, when he came down to his shop, the shoemaker could not believe his eyes. There on his workbench, where the leather had been, was the finest pair of shoes he had ever seen.

The shoemaker went to the stairs and called to his wife to come and see what he had found. "Did you make these shoes?" he asked her.

"Of course not," she replied.

The shoemaker was very puzzled and scratched his head in amazement. "Then who could it have been?" he wondered.

The shoemaker put the shoes in his shop window. That afternoon, a fine gentleman came to try them on. He liked the shoes very much, and gave the shoemaker a good price for them.

With the money, the shoemaker was able to buy food for dinner, and had enough left over to buy leather to make two new pairs of shoes.

Later that night, the shoemaker cut up the leather and left it lying on his workbench. "I'll finish the shoes in the morning," he yawned, shutting up the shop. He picked up the candle and went up the stairs to bed.

The next morning, when he came downstairs, the shoemaker was truly amazed. There, sitting neatly on his workbench, were two fine pairs of beautiful new shoes! They were soft and delicate. He thought they were the best shoes he had ever seen.

Once again, the shoemaker called his wife and asked if she had made them. "Oh, husband," she said, "of course I didn't."

The shoemaker was confused, but once again he put them in his shop window, where everyone could see them. In no time at all, he had sold both pairs for a very good price.

That evening, they had a marvellous dinner, and there was also enough money left to buy leather to make four new pairs of shoes!

Once more, the shoemaker cut out the leather and left it neatly on his workbench. And, in the morning, there were more new shoes waiting for him when he came downstairs. And so it went on for weeks. Every night the shoemaker cut out the leather and left it on his workbench, and every morning there were splendid shoes waiting to be sold. Soon the shoemaker and his wife were quite wealthy. But they still did not know who was making the smart shoes that appeared in the shop as if by magic.

One cold, wintry night, just before Christmas, the shoemaker and his wife decided that they had to solve the mystery once and for all. So, after the shoemaker left the leather on his workbench, he shut up the shop and hid in a big cupboard with his wife. They left the door slightly open so that they could see, and waited…

At last, when the clock struck midnight, there was a tiny noise from the dark chimney. It grew louder. Suddenly, two tiny elves appeared in a shower of magical stars. They ran straight over to the workbench and began to stitch and sew, until they had made five beautiful pairs of shoes.

They sang as they worked:

*"There isn't any time to lose,*
*We must make these fine new shoes!"*

As soon as the shoes were finished, they hopped off the workbench and shot up the chimney. The shoemaker and his wife were amazed and they wanted to do something in return for the kind elves. What could they do?

"They must be frozen in those thin, tattered clothes," said the shoemaker.

"Yes," said his wife. "And their feet are bare, although they make such beautiful shoes!"

So the shoemaker's wife made two little jackets and two pairs of trousers. She knitted four little woolly socks to keep their feet warm,

and two tiny hats for their heads. The shoemaker made two pairs of small boots, fastened with shiny silver buckles.

That evening, they wrapped the little clothes in tissue paper and left them on the workbench. Then they hid in the cupboard and waited …

At the stroke of midnight, there was a noise from the chimney and the elves appeared again. They were puzzled when they saw the parcels. But, when they opened all the presents, they were thrilled! They quickly put on their new clothes and danced. And as they danced, they sang happily.

They danced across the room, singing as they went –

*"See what handsome boys we are!*
*We will work on shoes no more!"*

Then they flew up the chimney and were gone in a flash!

The elves did not return, but the man and his wife never forgot the two tiny men and all their hard work.

And so the shoemaker continued to make shoes which were fine and beautiful, and he became rich and famous across the land. But none compared to the beautiful, light and delicate shoes that the little elves had made!

# Bone Crazy!

Alfie sat in his basket chewing on a large bone. Mmm! It tasted good. When he had chewed it for long enough, he took it down to the bottom of the garden, to bury it in his favourite spot. He didn't see next door's dog, Ferdy, watching him through a hole in the fence.

The next day, when Alfie went to dig up his bone, it was gone! Then he saw a trail of muddy paw prints leading to the fence, and he realised what had happened. Alfie was too big to fit through the fence and get his bone back, so he thought of a plan, instead!

Next day he buried another bone. This time, he knew Ferdy was watching him. Later he hid and watched as Ferdy crept into the garden and started to dig up the bone. Just then, Ferdy yelped in pain. The bone had bitten his nose! He flew across the garden and through the fence leaving the bone behind.

Alfie's friend Mole crept out from where the bone was buried. How the two friends laughed at their trick! And from then on, Ferdy always kept safely to his side of the fence!

# The Spooks' Ball

It is midnight and the spooks are going to the Annual Ball in the old Haunted Hall. By the light of the moon they will dance to a band that will play terrible tunes all night.

A spooks' band has instruments the like of which you will never have seen! The drums are made from skulls of all different shapes and sizes, the piano is made from the teeth of a dinosaur, and the violin is played with a bow made from cats' whiskers. But the strangest sound comes from the skeletons when they take to the dance floor. They shake their bones in time to the band, making a rattling tune which makes them howl with glee! In amongst the shaking skeletons is a witch dancing with her cat, but her boots are so big that she can't keep up with everyone else! A ghost with his head tucked underneath his arm is slowly feeding himself crisps.

As the sun rises the spooks all fade away and the Ball is over for another year – or have you been dreaming?

# The Haunted House

Have you ever been in a haunted house? No? Well, follow me and I will take you on a guided tour...

Step carefully through the rusty gates, but be quiet as a mouse, you don't want to upset the residents. Open the front door very slowly – otherwise it will creak and squeak, then everyone will know we are here. The hallway is full of ghosts wafting backwards and forwards, and look... some are walking through the doors when they are closed!

There are ghastly ghouls lurking on the stairs, and imps and sprites are having pillow fights. Look out – you will get covered in feathers!

Push open the kitchen door and a wizard is making slug and spider pies. I don't think we will stay to sample those when they are ready to come out of the oven!

Upstairs, skeletons are getting dressed and vampires are brushing their teeth. A suit of armour is getting in the bath – we won't stay in case he goes rusty!

So, an ordinary day in a haunted house – would you like to move in?

# Forever Friends

Daisy Duckling had lots of friends but her best friend of all was Cilla Cygnet. Every day they played together, chasing each other through the reeds. "When I grow up, I'll be a beautiful swan like my mummy!" said Cilla.

"And I'll be a dull little brown duck," said Daisy. She worried that Cilla would only play with her pretty swan friends when she grew up.

Then one day, they were playing hide and seek when something dreadful happened. While Daisy hid amongst some large dock leaves, a sly fox crept up and snatched her in his mouth! Before she had time to quack he was heading for his lair. But Cilla had been watching. She immediately rushed after the fox and caught the tip of his long tail in her sharp beak.

The fox spun round and Cilla pecked him hard on the nose. As his mouth dropped open, Daisy fell out, unhurt. Then Mrs Duck and Mrs Swan flew at him hissing loudly, and off he ran.

"That's what friends are for!" said Cilla. And Mrs Swan and Mrs Duck, who were the best of friends, could not agree more.

# The Chocolate Soldier

In the window of Mrs Brown's sweet shop there stood a chocolate soldier. He had chocolate ears and eyebrows and a curly chocolate moustache of which he was particularly proud. But best of all he loved his shiny foil uniform with its braid on the shoulders and cuffs, and smart red stripes down each leg. All day long the chocolate soldier stood to attention on a shelf in the window, staring straight ahead into the street. Standing next to him on the shelf were more chocolate soldiers, some lollipops, some sugar mice and a twist of liquorice bootlaces.

It was summer time and the sun shone through the window of the sweet shop. At first the chocolate soldier felt pleasantly warm; then he started to feel uncomfortably hot. Next he began to feel most peculiar indeed. His chocolate moustache was wilting and his arms were dripping. Soon he was completely melted and, before he knew it, he had slipped out through a hole in his silver foil shoe and was pouring off the shelf and out into the street.

Down the street he poured.

"Stop! Help me!" he shouted, but nobody could hear his cries.

Now he could hear the sound of gushing water and, to his horror, he could see he was heading for a stream at the bottom of the street.

"Help me! I can't swim! I'm going to drown!" the chocolate soldier cried as he plunged into the cold, running water. But now something very strange was happening – he found he could swim quite easily. He looked round and saw that he had a chocolate tail covered in scales. Then he looked at his arms, but there was a pair of fins instead. The cold water had hardened him into the shape of a chocolate fish!

The water carried the chocolate soldier until the stream broadened out and became a river. He realised that he would soon be carried out to sea.

"Whatever shall I do?" wondered the chocolate soldier. "I'm sure to get eaten by a bigger fish or maybe even a shark!" He tried to turn around and swim against the river's flow but it was no good. The current swept him away down river again.

Soon he could see the waves on the shore. He smelt the sea air and tasted the salt in the water. Now he found himself bobbing up and down on the sea. He could see a boat not far away and then all of a sudden he felt a net closing around him. He struggled to get out, but the net only tightened and soon he felt himself being hauled out of the water and landed with a "thwack!" on the deck among a pile of fish. The smell was awful, and the chocolate soldier was quite relieved when he felt the boat being rowed towards the shore.

"I'll hop over the side as soon as we land and run away," he thought, quite forgetting that he had no legs but only a fish's tail.

But there was no chance of escape. As soon as the boat reached the shore, he and all the other fish were flung into buckets and lifted into a van.

The van stopped outside a shop and a man carried the buckets inside, where it smelt of fried fish, chips and vinegar. The chocolate soldier found himself being lifted up with a lot of other fish in a huge metal basket. He looked down and saw a terrible sight below. They were heading for a vat of boiling oil! At that very moment he felt very peculiar once again. His scales melted, his tail drooped and he felt himself slide through the holes in the basket and into the pocket of a man's overalls.

The chocolate soldier lay in the corner of the pocket while the man worked in the shop. Then the man went home, with the chocolate soldier bouncing up and down in the overall pocket as the man walked along. Soon they arrived at the man's house. He reached into his pocket.

"Look what I've found," he said to his small son. "A coin. Here, you can have it – but don't spend it all at once!" he said, chuckling to himself. The chocolate soldier felt himself being passed from one hand to another.

"So now I've become a chocolate coin," he thought. "And I'm going to be eaten!" But to his surprise he was slipped into the boy's pocket.

The chocolate soldier felt himself bouncing up and down as the boy ran up the street and into a shop. The chocolate soldier peeped out and to his astonishment saw that he was back in Mrs Brown's sweet shop. The boy believed he was a real coin and was going to try and spend him!

The chocolate soldier called out to his soldier friends in the window, "Pssst! It's me! Help me!" One of the soldiers looked down, but all he could see was a chocolate coin sticking out of the boy's pocket. Then he recognised the voice.

"I'm a chocolate soldier too, but I've been turned into a coin. Help!" cried the chocolate soldier.

"Just leave it to me," replied the soldier on the shelf. "Don't worry, we'll have you out of there in a jiffy!"

The word was passed along and one of the sugar mice chewed off a length of liquorice bootlace. Then the soldier lowered the lace into the boy's pocket, where it stuck to the chocolate coin. Carefully the soldiers hauled the coin up on to the shelf. The chocolate soldier was delighted to find his foil uniform was still there on the shelf, just where it had been before. All the effort of getting on to the shelf had made him quite warm, and he found he could slip quite easily back through the hole in the shoe and into his uniform again.

"I'd like a chocolate soldier," said the boy to Mrs Brown. But when he reached in his pocket the coin had gone.

"Never mind," said kind Mrs Brown. "You can have one anyway." She reached into the window and took down a soldier from the end of the row and gave it to the boy. And as for our chocolate soldier? In the cool of the night he turned back into a smart-looking soldier again.

# Princess Rosebud

In a beautiful palace in a land far away, lived Princess Rosebud. She was named after the little pink mark on her ankle in the shape of a rose. On her third birthday, Princess Rosebud was given a pretty white pony which she rode with her nanny and her groom at her side. One day they went to the edge of the forest, then stopped for a rest. While the nanny and the groom talked together, the little princess wandered off to pick flowers. Soon Princess Rosebud was lost. She called and called for her nanny. No one came and the little princess was scared and began to cry.

Princess Rosebud walked on until she saw a light through the trees. There was a little house with a small wooden door. Suddenly, a little old woman opened the door. Now, the old woman was blind and couldn't see the little princess, but she could hear a small child crying. She took the little princess inside and sat her by a warm fire. Then she gave her thin slices of bread and honey, and a glass of milk.

"What is your name, child?" she asked.

"Rosebud," replied the princess. "I was picking some flowers, but I got lost in the forest."

The kind old woman told Rosebud that she could stay until someone came to find her. Rosebud was very happy living in the forest and forgot that she was a princess and had lived in a palace, and even forgot her white pony!

One day, when she was walking in the garden, a white pony appeared. Rosebud loved him immediately! She climbed into the saddle, and the pony galloped off. He took her to the palace and trotted through the gate as the king and queen were walking in the gardens. When they saw the little girl they thought she was the prettiest girl they had ever seen.

Just as Rosebud was mounting the pony to ride home, the queen saw, to her surprise, the pink rose on her left ankle!

"Sire!" she cried to the king. "It is our daughter, Princess Rosebud."

Rosebud realised where she was, and that the king and queen were her parents. She explained where she had been living and how the old woman had looked after her. The old woman was offered a reward for caring for the princess, but she said, "I only want to be near Rosebud for the rest of my days." So the old woman came to live in the palace with Princess Rosebud.

# Snow
# White

Long, long ago, in a faraway land, there once lived a king and queen who had a beautiful baby girl. Her lips were as red as cherries, her hair as black as coal and her skin as white as snow – her name was Snow White. Sadly, the queen died and years later the king married again.

The new queen was very beautiful, but also evil, cruel and vain. She had a magic mirror, and every day she looked into it and asked, "Mirror, mirror on the wall, who is the fairest one of all?" And every day, the mirror replied, "You, O Queen, are the fairest!"

Time passed, and every year Snow White grew more beautiful by the hour. The queen became increasingly jealous of her stepdaughter until one day, the magic mirror gave the queen a different answer to her question. "Snow White is the fairest one of all!" it replied. The queen was furious and at once invented an evil plan. She ordered her huntsman to take Snow White deep into the forest and kill her.

But the huntsman couldn't bear to harm Snow White. "Run away!" he told her. "Run away and never come back, or the queen will kill us both!" Snow White fled.

As Snow White rushed through the trees she came upon a tiny cottage. She knocked at the door and then went in – the house was empty. There she found a tiny table with seven tiny chairs. Upstairs there were seven little beds. Exhausted, she lay down across them and fell asleep.

Many hours later, Snow White woke to see seven little faces peering at her. The dwarfs, who worked in a diamond mine, had returned home and wanted to know who the pretty young girl was.

Snow White told them her story and why she had to run away. They all sat round and listened to her tale.

When she had finished, the eldest dwarf said, "If you will look after our house for us, we will keep you safe. But please don't let anyone into the cottage while we are at work."

The next morning, when the wicked queen asked the mirror her usual question, she was horrified when it answered, "The fairest is Snow White,

gentle and good. She lives in a cottage, deep in the wood!"

The queen was scarlet with rage because she had been tricked. She magically disguised herself as an old pedlar and set off into the wood to seek out Snow White and kill the girl herself.

That afternoon, Snow White heard a tapping at the window. She looked out and saw an old woman with a basket full of bright ribbons and laces.

"Pretty things for sale," cackled the old woman.

Snow White remembered the dwarfs' warning. But the ribbons and laces were so lovely, and the old woman seemed so harmless, that she let her in.

"Try this new lace in your dress, my dear," said the old woman. Snow White was thrilled and let the woman thread the laces. But the old woman pulled them so tight that Snow White fainted.

Certain that at last she had killed her stepdaughter, the queen ran through the forest to the castle, laughing evilly.

That evening, the dwarfs returned home. They were shocked to discover Snow White lying on the floor – lifeless. They loosened the laces on her dress so she could breathe and made her promise once again not to let in any strangers when they were at work.

The next day, when the mirror told the queen that Snow White was still alive, she was livid and vowed to kill her once and for all. She disguised herself and went back to the cottage.

This time the old woman took with her a basket of lovely red apples. She had poisoned the biggest, reddest one of all. She knocked on the door and called out, "Juicy red apples for sale."

The apples looked so delicious that Snow White just had to buy one. She opened the door and let the old woman in. "My, what pretty, rosy cheeks you have, deary," said the woman, "the very colour of my apples. Here, take a bite and see how good they are." She handed Snow White the biggest one...

Snow White took a bite and fell to the floor – dead. The old woman fled into the forest, happy at last.

This time, the dwarfs could not bring Snow White back to life. Overcome with grief, they placed her gently in a glass coffin and carried it to a quiet clearing in the forest. And there they sat, keeping watch over their beloved Snow White.

One day, as a handsome young prince rode through the forest, he saw the beautiful young girl in the glass coffin. He fell in love with her and begged the dwarfs to let him take her back to his castle.

At first the dwarfs refused, but when they saw how much the prince loved their Snow White, they agreed.

As the prince lifted the coffin to carry it away, he stumbled, and the piece of poisoned apple fell from Snow White's mouth, where it had been lodged all this time. Snow White's eyes fluttered open, and she looked up and saw the handsome young man.

"Where am I?" she asked him. "And who are you?"

"I am your prince," he said. "And you are safe with me now. Please will you marry me and come to live in my castle?" He leant forward and kissed her cheek.

"Oh, yes, sweet prince," cried Snow White. "Of course I will."

The next day, the magic mirror told the wicked queen of Snow White's good fortune. She flew into a rage and disappeared in a flash of lightning.

Snow White married her prince, and went to live in his castle. The seven dwarfs visited them often, and Snow White and her prince lived happily ever after.

# Smelly Pup

All the animals were gathered in the barn. "I have to tell you that we have noticed," said Mrs Hen to Smelly Pup, "that you are in need of a bath. You haven't had one all summer. Even the pigs are complaining!"

Smelly Pup just laughed. "Take a bath? That'll be the day!" he said.

Outside Smelly Pup strolled through the farmyard, muttering, "What a crazy idea. I'm a dog. I do dog things… like chasing cats!" The farm cat leapt up hissing as Smelly Pup came racing towards her. He chased her all around the farmyard. Then, just as he was about to catch up, she sprang into the air. Smelly Pup took a great leap after her… and landed in the pond with a SPLASH!

"Silly Pup!" smirked the cat as she watched from the branch of a nearby tree.

The ducks quacked as he spluttered and splashed, chasing them through the water! The water felt cool and refreshing on his fur. After a while, he came out and rolled on the nice muddy bank. "That was fun," he said. "Maybe I could get used to baths after all!"

# The Ant and the Grasshopper

Grasshopper was a lively, happy insect, who didn't have a care in the world. He spent the long summer days relaxing in the sunshine or bouncing and dancing through the grass. "Come and play!" he said to Bee one day.

"I'd love to," said Bee, "but I'm much too busy. If I don't gather this pollen, we bees won't be able to make honey. Then, when winter comes, we'll have nothing to eat."

"Well, work if you want to," said Grasshopper. "But I'd rather play!" And off he hopped. Then, Grasshopper saw Ladybird crawling along a leaf. "Come and play!" he called.

"Sorry, Grasshopper, not today," replied Ladybird. "I'm looking after the roses. They depend on us to guard them from greenfly!"

"Well, I think you're silly to spend this beautiful day working!" said Grasshopper, hopping away. Grasshopper went happily on his way, until he saw Ant, who was struggling to carry some grain on her back.

"Why are you working so hard?" asked Grasshopper. "It's such a sunny day! Come and play!"

"I have no time, Grasshopper," said Ant. "I have to take this grain back to my nest, so that my family and I have enough food when winter comes. Have you built your nest yet?"

"Nest?" laughed Grasshopper. "Who needs a nest when life in the great outdoors is so wonderful? And there's plenty of food – why should I worry?" And off he hopped.

At night, while the other insects slept, Grasshopper sang and danced under the moonlight. "Come and play!" he called to Spider, who was the only one awake.

"Sorry, Grasshopper," said Spider. "I have a web to spin. Can't stop now!"

"Suit yourself!" said Grasshopper, as he danced away. Day after day, Grasshopper played, while the other insects worked. And, night after night, he danced and sang while the others tried to sleep. The other insects were fed up.

"Stop that noise!" shouted Bee, one night. "You're keeping the whole hive awake!"

"Yes, be quiet!" said Ladybird.

As the summer went on, the long, sunny days began to get shorter and cooler. But lazy Grasshopper hardly noticed. He was still too busy enjoying himself. One day, Grasshopper saw Ant with her seven children. They were all carrying food back to their nest. "My, look at all your helpers," said Grasshopper.

"Well, we're running out of time," puffed Ant. "What are you doing about building a nest and storing food for the winter?"

"Oh, I can't be bothered," said Grasshopper. "There's lots of food around now, so why worry?"

That night, there was a chill in the air and Grasshopper didn't feel like dancing. "Maybe you'd better start getting ready for winter," warned Spider. It was getting colder, but Grasshopper didn't want to think about that now.

"Oh well, there's still loads of time for that!" said Grasshopper and he began to sing.

Soon the trees began to lose their leaves. Grasshopper was spending more time looking for food, but there wasn't much food to be found. One afternoon, Ant and her children scurried across his path, each carrying a fat, ripe seed. "Where did you find those?" asked Grasshopper, eagerly. "Are there any more?"

"There are plenty over there," said Ant, pointing. "When are you going to make a nest? Winter will be here soon!"

"I'm too hungry to think about that now," said Grasshopper, rushing towards the seeds and gobbling down as many as he could.

A few days later, it began to snow. Ladybird was in her nest, fast asleep. Bee was in her hive, sipping sweet honey with her friends and relations. Grasshopper was cold and all alone. He was hungry and he realised that there wasn't a crumb of food to be found anywhere!

"I know," said Grasshopper. "Ant will help me. She has plenty of food." So he set out to look for Ant's nest. At last, Grasshopper found Ant's cosy nest, safe and warm beneath a rock.

Ant came out to see him. "What do you want?" she asked.

"Oh, please, Ant," said Grasshopper, "do you have any food to spare?"

Ant looked at him, crossly. "All summer long, while my family and I worked hard to gather food and prepare our nest, what did you do?"

"I played and had fun, of course," said Grasshopper. "That's what summer is for!"

"Well, you were wrong, weren't you," said Ant. "If you play all summer, then you must go hungry all winter."

"Yes," said Grasshopper, sadly, as a tiny tear fell from the corner of his eye. "I have learned my lesson now. I just hope it isn't too late!"

Ant's heart softened. "Okay, you can come in," she said. "I will find some food for you, as long as you have really learned your lesson."

Grasshopper gratefully crawled into the warm nest, where Ant and her family shared their food with him.

By the time Spring came around, Grasshopper was fat and fit and ready to start building a nest of his very own!

# Hooray for Pepper!

**P**epper was a very noisy puppy. He wasn't a bad puppy. He was just so happy that he barked all day long.

"Woof! Woof!" he barked at the cat, at the birds, at the tree, and the postman, down the garden path.

One day, Pepper had been barking so much that everyone was trying very hard to ignore him.

"Be quiet, Pepper," said Jimmy, Pepper's little boy, as he lay on the lawn. "I can't concentrate on my book if you keep barking."

Pepper tried his very best not to bark. He tried to ignore the bright yellow ball lying on the path, he tried extra hard not to bark at the birds flying high up in the sky. But, everywhere he looked, there were things to bark at, so he decided to stare at the blades of grass on the lawn instead.

As he stared at the grass, Pepper was sure that it began to move. And as he carried on staring, Pepper was sure he could hear a strange slithering sound. He was just about to bark when he remembered Jimmy's words. He carried on staring.

Now he could hear a hissing sound. Pepper stared more closely, and then started to bark at the grass.

"Sshhh!" groaned Jimmy, as he turned the page of his book.

But Pepper didn't stop. He had spotted something long and slippery slithering across the lawn – something with a long tongue that hissed – and it was heading straight for Jimmy.

"Woof! Woof! WOOF!" barked Pepper, so loudly that Jimmy sat up, and looked around.

"Snake!" yelled Jimmy, pointing at the long slippery snake coming towards him. Pepper carried on barking as Jimmy's dad raced across the lawn and scooped Jimmy up in his arms.

Later, after the man from the animal rescue centre had taken the snake away, Jimmy patted Pepper and gave him an extra special doggy treat.

"Hooray for Pepper!" laughed Jimmy. "Your barking really saved the day." That night, Pepper was even allowed to sleep on Jimmy's bed.

And, from that day on, Pepper decided that it was best if he kept his bark for special occasions!

# Dino's Diner

There's a prehistoric venue that is open all day and night. It's the place where dinosaurs meet to catch up on the news, and have a bite to eat. But a bite for a dinosaur is rather large!

Dino's Downtown Diner is full to bursting with large, noisy dinosaurs. The triceratops call in to try the Diplodocus dips, and pterodactyls leave the sky for Dino's famous chips. Raptors are enraptured by the tasty deep-fried Lizard. There's Stegosaurus Steak and Brontosaurus Brunch, a massive Mammoth milkshake and a three course Caveman's Lunch. The huge plates are laden with hot and tasty food.

A word of warning though, in case you were thinking of visiting Dino's Downtown Diner one night. They have an extra special dish which, if you join the queue, might not be your idea of fun. Why? Because it's YOU!

# Monsters Everywhere

You can find monsters everywhere, if you know where to look! In the jungles and the valleys, in the cupboard under the stairs, in the bedroom and the kitchen – they are lurking everywhere.

In any lake, or pond or puddle, anywhere that fishes swim, you can be sure that lurking there is something rather grim. Trek up the highest craggy mountain where the snow lies all year long, listen to the silence and hear the yeti's song. If you gaze up into the depths of the starry night sky, you might glimpse a UFO. It could be from outer space, a traveller in time zooming towards earth to visit us. Hidden in the depths of the pyramids there are monsters galore, but beware! If you wake a sleeping mummy, it might come chasing after you!

But don't let this talk of monsters make you think it isn't safe to go out anywhere. A monster is part of our imagination. We can make them as horrible and revolting as we like! No one knows if they really exist – do they?

# A Home for Archie

Archie, the black and white kitten, wasn't pleased. His owner, Tessa, hadn't given him his favourite fish for breakfast. All he had in his dish when he looked was some biscuits left over from the day before.

"Out you go," said Tessa, who was busy mopping the kitchen floor. And she pushed Archie out the door. Now Archie was quite cross. He flicked his tail and swished his head. "I know when I'm not wanted," he thought. "I'll find someone who knows how to look after me!"

He jumped on to the garden fence and into the neighbour's garden. Mrs Green always gave him a treat. But, when his paws touched the ground, he heard a loud bark. Archie had forgotten about Bouncer, Mrs Green's playful new puppy. Bouncer raced across the lawn and started to bounce around Archie.

"It's far too rough here," thought Archie, scrambling up a handy tree. He jumped into the next garden. It belonged to Mr Reed. He didn't have a playful dog.

Archie strolled across the lawn and jumped up on to a window ledge. He was just about to squeeze through the

open window, when he heard a squawk,
followed by, "Who's a pretty boy?" Archie
had forgotten about Mr Reed's parrot.

"It's far too noisy here," thought Archie.
He made a quick escape through the hedge
to the next garden. Some new people had just
moved in and Archie hadn't met them yet. He hoped they liked kittens.
Archie strolled towards the house, but he hadn't got far when he heard
a hiss behind him. He turned around to see a Siamese cat preparing to
pounce. Archie didn't stop to say hello. He flew through the grass, leapt
on to the fence and ran as fast as his paws would carry him.

As he sat on the fence while he got his breath back, a wonderful fish
smell drifted past. Archie sniffed and followed his nose, his tail twitching
at the thought of a wonderful fish breakfast. Archie wandered past garden
after garden where children screamed, birds squawked, dogs barked and
cats wailed. At last his nose gave an extra big twitch and he stopped by
a garden that was wonderfully quiet.

"Archie, there you are!" a voice
called. It was Tessa. "I've finished
cleaning, and I've got a lovely piece
of fish for you!"

Archie purred. "Good old Tessa!"
he thought. "She does know how to
look after me, after all!"